I0689092

# SUMMER READ:

A desert island survival story

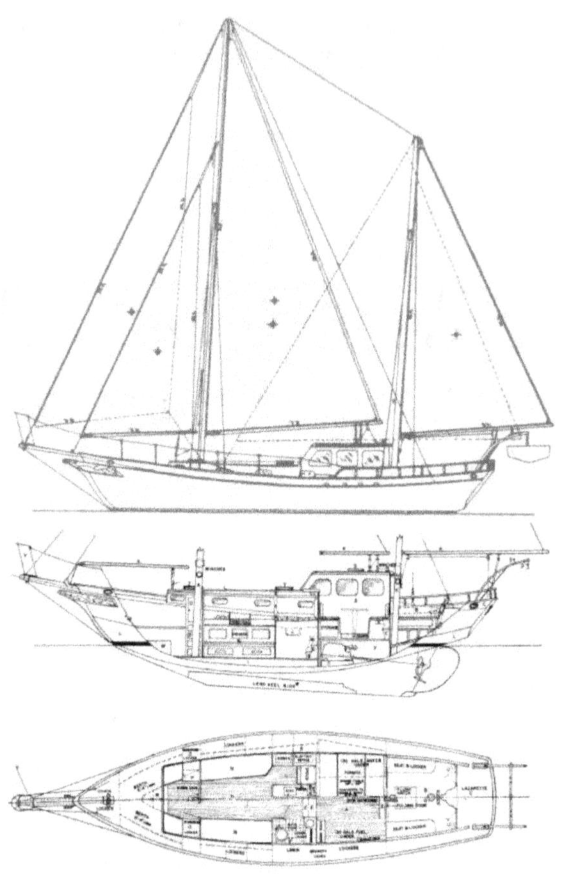

# Wham B'Ama

## Newporter 40 Pilothouse Ketch

# SUMMER READ:
## A desert island survival story

## Valerie Jones

Published by Valerie Jones
FLORIDA          ARIZONA

This book is a work of fiction. Names, characters, places and incidents are the product of the author's imagination or are used fictionally. Any relationship to actual events, locales, or persons, living or dead, is coincidental.

All rights reserved. In accordance with the U.S. Copyright Act of 1976, the scanning, uploading, or electronic sharing of any part of this book without the written permission of the publisher shall constitute unlawful piracy and theft of the author's intellectual property. If you would like to use material from the book (other than for review purposes) prior written permission must be obtained from the publisher at SilverLiningVal@hotmail.com.

Thank you for the support of the author's rights.

Copyright ©2025 by Valerie Jones-Long
All rights reserved

Dedicated to every woman and man who feared they would fail,

and to every woman and man who has beaten the odds.

Do what you dream.

We all fail.

And we all beat the odds.


And to J.T. Harris who spurred me to finally finish this book.

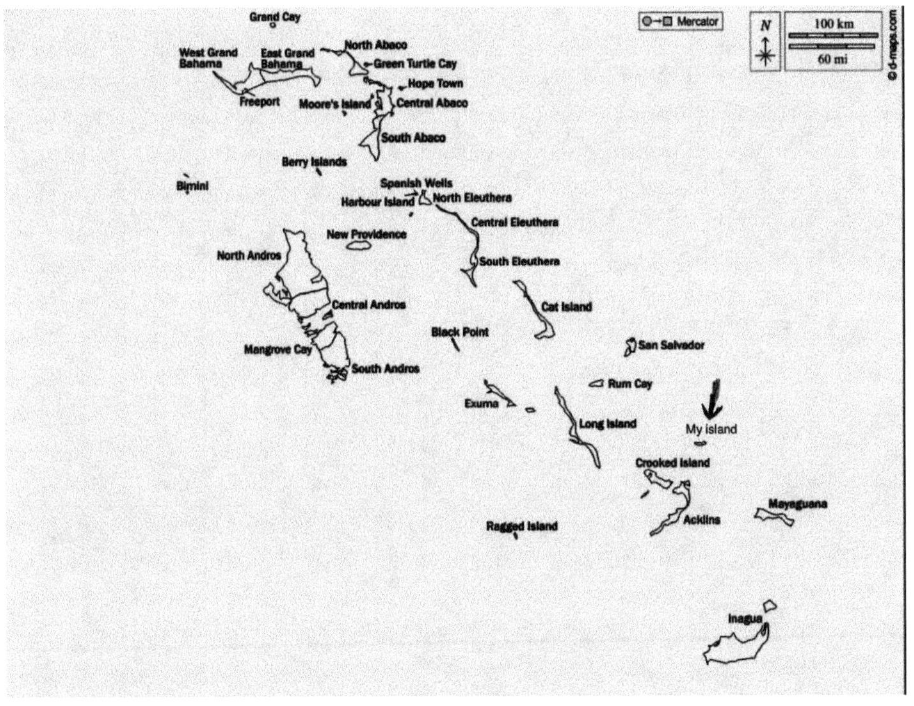


Thank you to D-Maps for this line drawing of the Bahama Islands. https://d-maps.com/carte.php?num_car=242158&lang=en

# ISLAND

# CHAPTER 1

## August 5, morning

A rough tongue scratches insistently at my left cheek. My throat is raw. My eyes are caked with sand. My right arm is pinned, numb, beneath me. Slowly, the ceaseless scraping of Raisin's tongue stirs me.

"Not on the mouth!" I grunt. Not even near drowning is enough to stifle my shudder as Raisin laps the sand from the edge of my mouth.

My God, I'm alive! I'm not dead or smashed to smithereens on the reefs or moonrock on this godforsaken island. I twist my neck, testing.

"You don't seem any the worse for wear, eh, Raisin? Where's Jim? Where's the boat?"

At the familiar name, Raisin looks down the beach but holds her ground. The wind is still howling past my ears, a cacophony of waves and surf drowning out my hoarse words. But the worst must be past.

Am I crippled?

Can I walk?

As I struggle to my knees, terror and questions flood my numbed brain. I peer through eyes that feel slashed with glass.

I'm on a dune — in a dune is nearer to it, I think. The air is alive with blowing sand and spume from the boiling sea. I'm covered with bits of brush and leaves that caught on me like a windrow. I'm a living tumbleweed.

I take stock. I scrape the hair off my face and try without luck to tuck the ends into the neck of my shredded yellow foul weather jacket clinging wetly to me. My hair — still long to my waist, despite protestations from friends who keep reminding me I'm too old, way too old, to keep it this length — is a mat of twigs and brush.

Eyes? Miraculously, one contact lens has stayed in place. It feels glued with sand and mucus, but I can make out distances. The little I can see is shrouded by blowing sand and hazed by salt spray. I'm an old-fashioned girl, and the contacts I wear are the original hard plastic ones. A real pain sometimes, not as convenient as the soft ones that stay in for a week, but a real blessing now. I can lick it clean, mostly, and it will keep me from bumping into walls. If there were walls.

Lower down? My arms and legs are bleeding from a million little cuts and scrapes, and my bruised body is one massive ache. My extra padding here and there — I only lied by 15 pounds on my driver's license — must have protected my ribs. Nothing feels broken.

As I snake out of my soaking nest, Raisin wriggles with excitement, dropping onto her front paws to lick again at my emerging face.

My arms and legs are in shreds, sliced and bruised by the rocks that miraculously spared my life. And Raisin's. But Jim?

The boat?

My personal inventory stops while I scan the teeming bay in front of me. The wind is still blowing too hard to peer into it. I manage to kneel upright, balancing my wavering torso against the debris protecting me, shielding my eyes and leaning into wind still nearly solid with airborne sand and fragments. How long since I reached the shore? I struggle to remember.

# STORM

# CHAPTER 2

# July 30

The wispy clouds foretold of danger. Jim and I, aboard our 40-foot sailboat, were spending the summer in the Bahamas, in the far far-out islands. We deserved a rest after spending two solid years restoring our classic boat from the bottom of her five-foot keel to the top of her 49-foot mainmast. She was a ketch, with two masts, a main and a mizzen, which we felt easier to handle, and safer than a sloop with just one mast.

It was hurricane season. We knew. We were in one of the worst spots we could possibly be, an isolated speck on the chart 150 miles from the nearest populated island. Populated by Bahamian standards: a booming metropolis of 12 families. We were 300 miles outside of radio range for weather forecasts.

We were also in a place where the water colors defied imagining, where the parrotfish and sea turtles and rays were so tame they headed over for a visit the second they spotted our toes entering the water.

Curlytails, the island's stocky lizards, ate their breakfast from our fingers and the shorebirds paraded their chicks past us like an Easter processional. The endless picture-postcard beach on the sheltered side of the island stretched pure and virginal every morning.

Raisin's racing paw prints joined barely perceptible indentations left by lizards and blowing leaves. The moonrock reefs on the ocean side of the island supplied a perpetual real-life video of iridescent fish and waving sea fans and corals.

We'd laugh. "God made the earth in six days. That was practice. Then he made the Bahamas." We were convinced. If there were a heaven on earth, this was it. Not even hurricane season could budge us.

We had seen the portentous wispy clouds twice earlier in the summer and rode out the storms they signaled. Each time the discussion was the same.

"Can we get the weather?" We were out of radio range of everything.

"Can we reach anyone who can get the weather?" Anyone we could reach had the same problem, or their forecast was a week old.

Other questions had no answers. Or no good ones.

"What if it's terrible?"

"If it's bad, where else can we go?"

"Can we get there in time if it is bad?"

"Which way is the storm headed?"

"Surely it won't come this way — let's stay tucked in here and chance it."

We knew from years of Florida summers that hurricane prediction is a crap shoot at best. You can break your neck getting ready for a storm that misses by 200 miles and passes with no more than a breath of wind. Or a hummer can form 50 miles away, foiling the weathermen, and you're dodging 90 knot gusts and 20 inches of rain in an afternoon. By the time they put a name to it, it's dissipated or 500 miles north. And the forecaster is still saying "... and a 20 percent chance of showers."

Over the weeks, then months, of staring at the sky and attempting our own predictions, we would each voice the fears, the questions, a dozen times, Jim reassuring me, me reassuring Jim, depending on which of us launched the litany.

With the early storms, we got lucky. The winds, when they came, peaked around 50, with gusts hitting 60 or 70 -- not as bad as the winter northers we'd suffered through in Florida and not nearly as cold.

After two tropical storms, Beatrice and Kevin, names we learned from friends passing through, we got cocky. Our island routine was unshakeable. Certainly not by a handful of telltale wisps out of the southeast. Certainly not by the glassy blue ocean tailor-made for our neophyte snorkeling and diving. Certainly not by the dog days of blinding heat without a breath of air and a sky that grew hazy and pale, with streaks of white so high we could barely make them out.

But then the days closed in, and the high clouds erased the stars to leave the nights pale and haunted. No. By the time we realized we could be in the path of a major hurricane, the questions were moot. It was too late to get anywhere or do much at all.

For a few days we'd noticed high, high wisps of cloud stretching across the blue sky.

Normally, they'd signal a thunderstorm the next day. But these clouds persisted and grew wider. The air stilled and grew even more humid. This was real trouble.

On this day the heat drove us early from our beds. Yes, beds. Plural.

We were partners in the boat, and partners in pursuing this island life but the enforced intimacy and stresses of years shared in an area smaller than a parking space at the mall had long before ended the few traces of romance our relationship had started with six years before.

Once, driving through Texas, we told a chatty waiter we lived on a sailboat. He cooed, "How romantic! You must really like each other a lot!" Jim and I looked at each other, struck dumb at the thought.

Finally, I spoke. "I think it's more a question of being able to tolerate one another fairly well." A shining example that my notorious lack of tact is exceeded only by my almost total scarcity of subtlety.

That's what 40 years in the newspaper business will do for you. No defense attorney would ever want me. Not a sympathetic bone left.

So as the summer waned, our days passed largely in our separate solitudes, Jim's and mine. Our little heaven on earth had flaws. Twenty times a day, I would ask myself, "What on earth am I doing here? With this person?"

The simple answer was that I had my life savings tied up in the boat. I had no job, no prospects, and no way to get my money out, short of a miraculous upturn in the used boat market. The upside was, like I told the waiter, we could tolerate each other.

Simple as that. He had to live with my snoring, and I had to endure his peeing in a coffee cup 25 times a day. And his smoking.

Often, I'm sure, we aggravated the shit out of each other, but quietly. I learned not to tell him when he was doing a project all wrong and it wouldn't hold up, and simply wait for the explosion when it didn't.

He grew tolerant of my exploring that would take me off for hours at a time while I indulged in bird-watching or people-watching, equally fascinating and educational. Largely, we lived alone together, putting a better face on it from time to time when family visited or one of us resolved to improve things.

On a typical day, Jim would wake first and struggle into the cockpit with his coffee and yet another trashy war novel. And a new pack of smokes.

I would stretch and snooze for a bit longer, then savor my first coffee before venturing anything complicated, like speech. Our conversations dealt largely with the weather and food.

"Looks like a nice day, finally."

"I hate to commit this early." Optimism was not his strong suit.

Or, "We're almost out of canned milk, maybe two weeks left, tops. We'll have to make a supply run."

A supply run meant 150 miles upwind to St. George's Harbour, a bustling community of a dozen families.

The grocery store constituted three sparsely stocked shelves propped on concrete blocks next to an ancient RCA television in a two-room shack cluttered with dogs and children. The freight boat stopped every two weeks to deliver orders called in to their relay station.

The trip in each direction was a sailor's nightmare. In a car, a pleasant couple of hours. But in a boat, at three or four miles an hour, not so much. We gritted our teeth against the prospect, stomped our feet, and only gave in to making the trip when we were desperate. Like when Jim ran out of cigarettes.

Southbound, we'd fight all the way to keep the sails drawing in a measly five knots of wind dead astern. That meant the cockpit was still as a sauna, and we'd be drenched in sweat.

If we motored, the sails would collapse and we'd roll rail to rail, and suck diesel fumes for 30 hours. Without the motor we made a painful 2 or 3 miles an hour, doubling the time for the trip.

Slow or fast — fast being a relative term at 5 or 6 knots — it was an eternity of a trip.

If we chose a blistering motorboat ride, rocking and rolling in the swells, exhaust smoke swept into the cockpit. It was like eating New York City bus fumes from from Maine to California.

Wiping sweaty soot off my face and onto my ruined tee shirt and watching my white cockpit cushions blacken into thrift shop rejects, I'd think, This is the part the cruising magazines leave out.

Invariably, when the wind did pick up, it would be from the direction we were headed. We'd labor into an uncomfortable chop that pitched salt spray onto the decks and forced every window closed and bolted.

# STORM

# CHAPTER 3

# August 1, morning

But that day, the last day I remember clearly, there was no question of motoring off for supplies, or motoring off anywhere. The air was thick and gluey. It clung like wet dough to the skin.

The ocean was oily, slack, ominous. The bay gleamed like the proverbial mirror. The sun never rose. The eastern sky just paled to a white on white dome. To the south, we could see the very tops of clouds portending huge boiling cumulus a hundred miles distant.

We took one look and started working together, something that, most of the time, we did well. We didn't need words, just strength and speed. We stripped off the awnings first, huge expanses of heavy fabric that kept the boat shady and cool. We rolled and tied the bundles before taking them below.

The 30-foot PVC pipes we used to hold them out were too long to fit anywhere inside the boat except on the cabin floor, so we would have to step lively once we were shut up inside.

I cursed those damn poles a thousand times, every time I tripped and every time they moved and rattled and flew around and got in the way. But by then it was too late.

Next came the mainsail, a huge spread of canvas it took both of us to carry. We flaked and rolled and folded it as best we could, then struggled to drag it off the pilothouse roof and into the cockpit. We were nearly dead of the heat by the time we manhandled it through the cabin door and into the v-berth, where it took up an entire bunk.

Next came the mizzen, nearly as long as the main at its base but 15 feet shorter. It slid out of the sail track in a heap onto the floor of the cockpit, and we bundled it up and crammed it onto the bunk next to the main.

The jib was already bagged — we'd been lazy sailors — and we managed to cram it through the forward hatch into the overflowing V-berth. We wouldn't be sleeping in those bunks, I thought… but we probably wouldn't be sleeping anyway.

Only the staysail was left, a tiny sail really, intended to save the boat in a storm, or steady her. Alone, it's the last-ditch sail seasoned sailors called a handkerchief. It can steady a boat in perilous winds. I wanted to leave it on. Jim wanted it struck and taken below with the rest.

I confess. I'm compulsive about few things on the boat but safety, or what I perceive as safety, is one.

"What do you think about leaving the staysail rigged and ready to hoist?" I ventured, tempering my normally more direct approach as best I could in response to years of Jim's complaints that I try to order him around.

"No. Get it off the deck. Everything has to go. Get it below."

"I think we should leave it rigged. What if we need it?" I stand my ground.

Jim throws the screw gun he's using onto the deck and starts forward.

"I have to do every goddam thing. I'm the only one who ever worries about this boat's safety." He begins a speech I've heard dozens of times.

I give in and pull the bronze fasteners to release the sail, then feel a breath of wind. It riffles the tangled hair at the back of my neck and the sweat pouring down my back turns icy cold with fear. I glance up and see the mass of cloud towering higher now. Below it, like a black fineline marker, the kind accountants use, the storm wall.

Exhausted, we stopped for a coffee, reminded again that we had less than a week's supply of milk — canned, dried or otherwise — and now we were bound to run out.

We munched bread and butter because there was no time for sandwiches or cereal. The fine black line on the horizon ripened into a pencil smudge, growing thicker and wider before our eyes.

Perched halfway up the mast with the good Zeiss binoculars, we could see waves on the horizon, little hillocks of water like miniature snowcapped mountains. From this distance, they didn't look fierce.

The ocean had an oily motion of with swells growing closer together. The stillness and silence were eerie. No bird cries or slap of waves on the boat. We felt suddenly deaf.

While I bagged the tiny staysail, Jim resumed screwing plywood onto the cabin sides to protect the beautiful pilothouse windows that had gone a long way toward making us fall in love with the boat. Beautiful but vulnerable, nine windows, each nearly three feet wide, on the three sides of the pilothouse.

Neither of us voiced the dread of the growing black line on the horizon. It forewarned of our own personal Hurricane Ian. We had seen the wreckage of that terrible storm, and the thousands of demolished buildings, miles of snapped and lifeless trees.

Now we were the crickets who hadn't taken proper care. We were slaving to try to catch up. Too late. Too little.

A rippling blue carpet overtook the glassy sea to lead a first frigid whisper straight to us. We glanced away from the work for an instant, our eyes locked in a silent prayer for the storm to veer.

I was lashing the main boom down, using every trick I knew to make it tight and solid on top of the cabin. Basically, the boom was a 40-foot tree, nearly a foot in diameter at the mast slimming to eight inches where it nearly touched the mizzen mast.

Years before, Jim had finally retired the argument, "I am man. I tie knots. I tie down! Ug!" It had been a constant amazement to me, in the first years we were together, that a man who'd spent half his life in the Army couldn't put out a tarp that didn't flap like a strangled chicken in the slightest breeze.

And he still had to mouth to himself every time he tied a bowline knot, "The rabbit goes around the tree..." And I could always see him say, "This tree? No, this tree." So I did the tarps and tiedowns and knots, especially when it mattered. And it mattered now.

Jim started screwing\ boards to the cabin side to protect the smaller windows. Thanks to the rebuild we had done, we still carried enough scrap wood on board to open a lumberyard. I watched, and resisted suggesting slicing up some vinyl and screwing that on for protection as well. Better to be dark and blind inside the boat than sprayed with broken glass and deluged with whatever followed.

Another hour later and the wind had freshened and cooled so we were no longer sweating from the heat, just from the exertion. A mixed blessing. The smudge on the horizon was a child's angry crayon slash, whitecaps boiling beneath it. Wham B'Ama, the crazy name we had given the boat, nudged gently against the smaller of the two anchors, a Danforth that we hoped was halfway to China after weeks in the same spot.

We would pay out nearly all of the 300-foot one-inch braid I called the firehose. And we would let out the rest of the 200 feet of heavy chain attached to the big anchor, the 65-pound CQR which had rested peacefully on deck even during our tropical storms. But not this time.

We even got the ancient fisherman's anchor ready to load into the Whaler. It's attached to 30 feet of huge half-inch chain that I can only lift five links at a time. It's shackled to the spare 300 foot anchor line I had stored in the back of beyond, deep in the bowels of the aft compartment, for just such a terrifying moment.

"If we have it, we'll never need it," I'd said two years before when I bought the heavy spool of rope. Like knocking on wood, or not stepping on a sidewalk crack. I got it for a rainy day. Looking at the sky and at our meager efforts to save our boat and ourselves, I know the rainy day is now.

In the midst of this, Raisin barks to go ashore.

"Maybe later. Maybe later," I shout over the rising wind. "Maybe later."

# ISLAND

# CHAPTER 4

# August 6, early afternoon

"Later, not right now," I mumble, shielding my exposed ear from her demanding yelp. An insistent paw threatens to make mincemeat of my already flayed fingers.

I'm asleep. I'm not getting ready for the storm. I'm getting over it. Raisin's bark is a warning that the waves are edging perilously close to my nest. I lean into my dune, nature's lounger, I think.

Heaps of sodden seaweed engulf tattered sea grape to make a soft resting place. I peer around. The wind has slacked. I can open my eyes.

Raisin nudges her head under my chin. Her presence is an unspeakable comfort, a sign that all is not lost. It appears that I tumbled with other detritus on the storm surge onto the island's highest dune, barely protected from the wind and fierceness of the waves.

But protected just enough. A scant 20 yards further along this beach and I would never have survived.

I would have been impaled on coral spikes as sharp as razors and pounded to so many pieces not even the sharks would notice.

I remember the questions. The boat? Jim? Where are they? I focus on the white-capped bay. The familiar landmarks are gone. The big trees are down, those standing look like winter ghosts stripped of every leaf.

The spume is littered with branches, trunks, leaves, and wave after wave of fragments smaller than a shred of oatmeal. This brown confetti is everywhere, in the water, in the air, on the beach, like the whole world made a quick trip through the Cuisinart.

It's still blowing 30 at least, I think. But I can maneuver in this. I struggle to my bleeding knees and grasp Raisin's back. She's used to being a crutch for these old bones.

"I'll make it up to ya, kid," I snarl, my throat raspy from sand and salt water. I reach my feet and she bounds along the tiny ribbon of flying sand left by the rising tide, her paws sinking in the saturated dune, then racing back for me to follow. A fragment of normality in chaos, I think…

I try to follow Raisin, but the sand is impossible. I sink past my ankles, and the water spraying against my legs is a burning reminder of my frail condition. I move away from the edge and sit down, collapsing the sand beneath me with no seagrape to cushion the drop.

I have to take stock. The dog and I made it, she clearly better than I. Where is Jim? With the boat? Where is the boat? Was I washed overboard? Did we sink? Does anyone in the world know where I am? Or that I'm alive? Is he?

I scan the horizon, but it's still too hard to look into the wind. I try to shield my eye with the contact lens so I can see but I'm terrified it will blow away. Then I'd really be in trouble. Rescue would have to tap my shoulder for me to know it was here. I'd have to trip over Jim to find him— or the boat.

We should have painted her red, I think. Not blue, for chrissakes. She might as well be invisible. "Like you," I shout at Raisin. "The boat should have big red spots, just like you." She takes my words as an invitation and bounds chest deep through the raging water to deliver a stick. "Be careful out there," I warn her, just like the sergeant on Hill Street Blues.

"What the hell am I saying? You've made it this far."

# STORM

## CHAPTER 5

## August 1, afternoon

Jim lashed the Whaler to the side of the big boat and duck-walked the huge yachtsman anchor to the edge of the deck. Getting it into the Whaler was a massive challenge. Both boats were pitching now, and the the timing had to be perfect.

I dropped into the smaller boat to help hold it steady while Jim eased the anchor over the edge of the deck. When the Whaler felt the weight, it tipped and nearly dumped me and the anchor but I held on with every ounce while Jim directed the shank onto the floor and the anchor followed.

We switched places and I let out the chain and heavy line as he backed away from the boat.

He only managed 80 feet against the growing wind before he tossed a tiny anchor to hold his place while he dumped the yachtsman. There was no way to control the drop or to set it, but it was down. It was our insurance. That was the plan. The other two anchors should hold us fine.

## August 1, late afternoon

Jim was behind me, strips of a torn sheet -- chafing gear -- whipping from his hand like outraged snakes. He leaned forward into the blasting wind and dropped to his knees as he reached the foredeck. He wrapped and tied the pieces of cloth around and around the exposed anchor rode so if line had to be released, it would still be protected. I watched his fumbling hands, the tendrils of sheet whipping now out of the waistband of his shorts.

He's tying grannies again. Nothing to do about it now. As I turned, I looked up and over my shoulder at the sky. Black. With a roiling gray-green underbelly the color of long-forgotten copper. In the distance an invisible line divided frenzied whitecaps from an approaching maelstrom.

"Jim! Jim!" I shouted hopelessly over the pilothouse roof. There was no chance he'd be able to hear me. I stepped over the coaming onto the deck and grabbed the rigging as I eased myself forward into shouting range.

I reached the cabin roof and sat down, my fingers curling into the mahogany handrails and scooting sideways toward Jim's figure crouched beside the windlass. As I reached the halfway mark, he glanced up and glared.

We had long used hand signals and there was no mistaking his jabbing finger. He wanted me to go back to the cockpit.

I shook my head and pointed forward, then arced my finger up and over the black dome of sky and jabbed toward the boil of surf rapidly approaching the boat.

Even though the bay was sheltered by island standards, the sand dunes topped by Australian pines offered little protection for the approaching winds and rain.

Jim's eyes widened to the size of saucers. He glanced back and nodded, jabbing again at the back of the boat. I nodded back, and dropped to all fours to crawl back to the cockpit.

The wind was worse just in the last two minutes. I tried to remember wind strengths and the damage they wrought.

The worst I'd been out in was 70 miles an hour and it nearly blew me backward off the dock. Now I was on a bucking platform.

Could I stand? Why try? Just because my teeshirt is blowing off my body with the bottom up around my ears? So what? Give 'em one last thrill.

After all, the boobs are still darn good. If anybody out there cares. God, what am I doing thinking about boobs now? I could be dead tomorrow.

ISLAND

CHAPTER 6

August 6, morning

But I'm not dead. Alone, but alive. I should be terror-stricken, petrified, I think. Ye gods, all those overstated verbs I had to use when I was writing those crazy survivor stories at the Globe, one of those horrible tabloids at supermarket checkout lines.

"Yes, Mr. Jones, and just how did it feel as the tornado sucked you out of your tent and swept you 200 feet off the ground and across the river? You didn't feel anything, you say?

"Weren't you petrified? Didn't you see your life pass before your eyes? Didn't you say to yourself, 'Please God, don't let me die?' Mr. Jones, didn't you think those things? Yes? Good..."

And "Mrs. Smith, wasn't it the worst moment of your life when you saw your son's blazing body catapult out of the 6th story window? Mrs. Smith? Are you there?"

The supermarket tabloids are always happy to clarify those peak life experiences. God, what a soul-sucking seven years that was, reducing the most dramatic and painful of human experiences to the lowest common denominator of our readers. Not to mention our editors.

Better here, stranded, alone, than back there pounding out mile after mile of insincere copy. Maybe when I get back, I can do a first person. Let's see, how does that go? "Please God, don't let me...."

# STORM

# CHAPTER 7

# August 1, afternoon

I pulled my teeshirt away from my face long enough to make sure Jim was leaving the deck. He stood braced a few feet behind me, knees and feet wedged between two shrouds - the wire rigging that attaches the mast to the deck - as he adjusted his shorts. That better have been sea spray I was feeling, I groused to myself. Nerves. How about sheer terror?

Jim's bladder was as good as any storm warning system. What did he tell me? That he peed 37 times in the hour it took him to get through Hell's Gate in New York?

I hope he brings a big cup with him into the cabin. Once we're in, we're in.

While Jim finished clearing the decks, I went inside to get everything movable stowed or shoved away or lashed down.

Wham B'Ama was a Newporter 40, custom made in 1965 for an unnamed California movie star.

She was the prettiest boat I could ever imagine, and super comfortable to live on.

In the cockpit, all the way at the back, she had what they called the Queen's Couch, a big expanse of seat bigger than a king size bed.

Rather than reclining, we put folding chairs up there for cocktails and the evening S-and-S, Sitting and Staring. We'd stare at other boats, other people, the water, the sunset, the changing palette of color, all better than the best PBS nature special.

On each side of the cockpit was a roomy locker/seat as wide as a cot and more than 6 feet long, great for the night watches, even better for parties.

The mizzen mast stood tall next to the offset door, the mizzen boom perfectly placed to hold an awning over the cockpit. The door into the pilot house was a real door, bi-fold teak with Lexan windows. One broad step led inside. No ladder!

Inside the pilothouse, a big six-seater dinette occupied the right side. It was raised to allow for a big chart drawer underneath and for good visibility out of the nine big windows.

Two broad mahogany steps led down to the main salon - the living room. On the right was the u-shaped galley, with a huge double sink, a fridge and freezer, lots of drawers and cabinets, even a bread maker. Opposite the galley was the bathroom, roomy with a big shower. Now the shower was jammed with everything that would fit in there - ropes, bags of books, pillows - an assortment of soft things that could be piled and crammed into the shower, a milk crate with extra supplies impossible to find in the distant islands.

The big settee dominating the main salon flipped open to be a double bed, and the opposite side held a small seat with a closet behind. A big leather trunk sat between, good for a footrest or holding snacks and drinks. Wham B'Ama had storage everywhere — below and behind the settee, beneath the dinette seats, in the walls.

We had found custom-made varnished mahogany drawers and matching louvered doors stripped from a 120-foot yacht. We adapted them for Wham B'Ama's interior. She was spectacular.

The huge V-berth that we clambered into at night was nine feet wide at the head end, tapering to three feet wide at the feet. A closed locker at the foot of the bed held the chain and rope for the two main anchors.

Under Jim's side of the V-berth was a 60-gallon tank for fresh water, and under my side was a massive space for storage. We used it for dog food. We started the cruise with eight 40-pound bags of Purina, each sealed in doubled contractor trash bags to keep them dry and bug free.

# August 1, late afternoon

So now my job is to pack everything that had been dragged in from the outside of the boat into the inside, and still leave it livable. Tall order.

The clouds on the southern horizon had grown into towering mountains, 40,000 feet high, but we were only seeing the top quarter. The cloying heat had dropped another 10 degrees in the last hour and the black band of the storm's leading edge stretched all across the horizon.

The awning and poles already dominated the floor and were too long to move anywhere else. I grabbed the man-overboard bag, the life jackets, the horns, and set them near the steps, ready for a quick getaway. I tried to leave access for the galley. It was dark inside the boat, and stifling hot.

Jim had secured more canvas over the hatches to try to keep the coming rain out. The inside of the boat was like a steaming sweat lodge. I worked with the help of one cabin light.

I knew it could be a while before we ran the motor to charge the batteries, and we would need the battery power for our instruments and the radio when this was over.

If this gets over, I thought.

Raisin had ensconced herself in her usual cave, under the table in the pilothouse. Good.

Out of the way.

I glanced around at the ruin that was the inside of our pretty boat. The table and dinette were heaped with spare line. In my few trips in and out, the cockpit awning had already started unrolling from its PVC pipes, and the tiedown lines hurled a knotted frenzy at my ankles as I tried to pick my way past.

I grabbed a canvas bag and shoved in the loose books and charts already strewn about the cabin. I stripped the curtains from the darkened windows and carried the bundle forward to join the sails. I made another pass at the pilothouse, gathering up the line in one heap and doublechecking the windows. Tape wouldn't hurt, I thought, grabbing the duct tape and ripping a giant X across each pane. I tucked fresh towels in the proven leaky spots, knowing it was futile.

I dropped the two steps into the main salon and galley. Another canvas bag. Loose plates, glasses, cups. Save two big mugs out for coffee and soup, I thought.

Soup? Who are you kidding? I remembered what we went through in a surprise blow on vacation in the Abacos. Ha! You'll be lucky to gnaw on a hunk of cheese and sliced salami. I checked the refrigerator for cheese and salami, and made sure munching food was near the top.

Maybe better in a bag? No. I'll bag it if it gets rough.

I swept books, CDs, tapes, mementoes off the big pilothouse shelf and into more bags. When I ran out of canvas, I switched to plastic. In my frenzy, I started muttering out loud. "Paper or plastic? Just like home -- almost."

I clipped on a snug new bungee cord to hold the big cabinet doors and cleared the shelf behind the settee. All books. Better wrapped in plastic.

It will take me weeks to put everything back, I think to myself. "That's the least of your worries." My inner voice escaped.

"What did you say?" Jim swept into the cabin.

"Nothing, just looking at the mess. Should we close the seacocks? Can we reach anyone at all to let them know to check on us?"

No answer. Of course. He left as quickly as he came in, exhaling smoke. His lighter wouldn't stay lit in the growing breeze, thus the brief visit inside. The thunderheads, still 50 miles away, towered so high we felt like ants. The black crayon line of the front dominated the horizon, and wispy tendrils of cloud dropped out of the sky in the deadly dancing lines we knew were waterspouts. Closing in. I counted six.

I felt the wind shift. I peered around the main salon again. We did great work, I thought for the thousandth time. The varnish gleamed in the lamplight.The wallpaper added just enough color to relax the formal "yachty" look.

Not that the clutter didn't manage that well enough. The blue moire taffeta slip covers took on almost every color of the sea, never the same twice. Except this color, I thought. It's never been this color, this terrifying iron gray.

We did it all. We wrapped the lines with actual firehose and tied it on so it wouldn't wear through. We debated trying to hide the boat in the mangroves and tying off to the trees, but time dictated that we were committed to stay put. The minutes left had to go to securing the boat where she was. And securing ourselves inside her. We could die.

# ISLAND

# CHAPTER 8
# August 6, afternoon

I gather my strength and edge inland from the sodden dune. The island is saturated, standing water everywhere, everything a mushy soup of sand, tattered leaves, smashed twigs. Bits of plastic and white styrofoam and colorful plastic bottle caps punctuate acres of brown ooze. Naked trees lift abbreviated branches to the whipping sky.

My reef shoes are still on my feet. Thank the lord, I think, something that lives up to the ads. The goo sucks at my ankles as  I wade along the unfamiliar coast. My insides feel hollow.   Hunger or shock? Fear of the future or thrill of survival?

The wind is steadily dropping, but the crashing wavetops still fly past my protective dune. This way is pointless. I walk a few more sucking steps. Pointless. Sodden beach and ooze.

I turn and head for the moonrock. The 100 yards to the first solid rock plunders the little strength I had when I awoke.

 Even Raisin slowed. She senses my destination and closes the gap to play king of the mountain before I reach the halfway mark. She sprawls, ears at full alert, panting while I catch up.

As I struggle, the ferocity of the waves seems to subside, the crashing not quite so loud, the spume not so brutal. High tide? I squint at the sun, just off-center above the swirling clouds.

Afternoon, not morning, I think. But early afternoon.

"I need to remember this, Raisin! Raisin! Write that down. High tide is early afternoon. Remind me." Raisin's sand-shrouded eyes gleam at me and she wags her tail.

She's heard my ravings  before. It's all good fun. In a fluid motion, she gains her feet and leaps over the moonrock to greet me.

I look around. The bluff I'm on is a scant 10 feet above the waves, with surf foaming nearly to the top of my perch. The bluff I had hiked these weeks past stood 30 feet above the water, at least,  with wizened palmettos and scrub clinging to the highest crags. I  barely recognize this rock.

I grab the black, jutting moonrock with tender hands and scramble by inches up and away from the  deafening surf. The noise! What I wouldn't give for a minute of quiet.

I look at Raisin, busy gnawing on a fallen branch from a tree that had survived a hundred hurricanes before this dog attacked it.

"Give it a rest," I shout, edging my sore and aching butt onto a skillet-sized expanse of flat rock. I perch with jagged rocks threatening to pierce my right thigh if I wiggle even a silly millimeter.

I survey again. The wind is definitely dropping, the ominous clouds whipping by are taking on a fluffy appearance, and the boil of water in the bay is definitely subsiding.

On the ocean side, huge mountainous waves on the horizon resemble wriggling pinking shears. Behind me, the moonrock extends out and up.

Exhausted leafless trees look like abandoned kindling. On the bay side, the water was releasing its grip on the soggy sand to reveal a mucky, littered beach. In front, the wicked waves seemed less set on destruction.

Raisin was the only living thing I could see. She was the only one who knew I was here. I was more alone than I'd ever been in my life.

# STORM

# CHAPTER 9

# August 1, afternoon

I stepped over the marine store goldmine that had been our pretty salon and joined Jim in the cockpit. He was jamming a strip of vinyl onto the instrument panel, in the sure belief that one little tuck would hold it against the coming winds.

I took it from his hand and grabbed a piece of line to secure it with a bowline and a trucker's hitch. He stared at my handiwork as though it were magic.

We couldn't decide about the Whaler. Take it to shore and lash it and ourselves to a tree? Leave the Whaler tied to the big boat? Take it ashore and risk swimming back?

Where is Johnny Weismuller when you need  him? No decision made that decision. It stayed lashed to the boat on the longest floating line we had. We prayed it wouldn't tangle with an anchor or get picked up and come soaring into the  cockpit.As we stood there, we heard a distant moan of the approaching wind, like a starving beast emerging from its den after a long winter.

The solid black band, now like a crayon slash, split the ocean and sky and the most monstrous clouds I'd ever seen blotted out the rest. Shards of lighting raced through the clouds, still too far to hear the crack.

At the edge of our vision the water was alive, like a bubbling cauldron. Spray flew off the crests and raced ahead of the wind like a frightened cat. My tee shirt whipped my body, and my sweat-gummed hair threw its tendrils to the wind.

Wham B'Ama snugged up on the heavy anchor line and I again thanked the inventor of braid on braid rope. The anchor line was as thick as a garden hose. It could move a skyscraper.

The wind snapped our faces like a wet towel and the rigging took up the wail. This  was just the beginning.

# ISLAND

# CHAPTER 10

# August 6, afternoon

I struggle up. "Raisin! Where are we? Where's lunch? Food? Let's get serious here!" Raisin scampers away from a mound of draining debris trapped against an outcropping and heads my way, panting from her exertions.

Her vocabulary is impressive. "Food" was one of her earliest words and she always gives great thought to questions pitched her way. Any answer is fine with her. One of the great things about a dog, not like a person, I think.

Food is a definite priority. Most of the time, but especially now. I know I should have actually read that book: Edible Bahamian Wild Plants. Damn, I never even looked at it before I jammed it onto the bookshelf in the main salon. I wonder where it is now?

How long has it been since I've eaten? Since we'd eaten? Where was the boat? Where am I? Every labored step across the slowly drying moonrock brings a new torrent of questions. Not just about how I'm to survive or reach civilization, but about how I got here.

The sun blazes low through the scudding clouds and steam rises steadily from the saturated rock and sand. I strip off my shredded foul weather jacket and push up the sleeves of the dripping sweatshirt beneath.

Blood from scrapes and scratches spreads like ugly watercolors. My sturdy denim shorts seem none the worse for wear, just gummy and sand-encrusted. I roll the jacket into a solid ball and poke it into a niche in the rock to pick up on the return trip, then add the sweatshirt. I'm in hunting mode.

# STORM

# CHAPTER 11

# August 1, early evening

Dog food! It's buried under the goddam V-berth.

Raisin is a 70-pound mutt. We tell people she's a liver spotted Dalmatian, but she has enough pit bull in her genes that she fulfills her duty as chief guard dog better than we could have wished.

She does too well at times. We have to keep a watch on her with kids. She likes them well enough for lunch.

She's solid, wiry muscle from stem to stern. I suspect a whippet might be an uncle somewhere. In the Bahamas, the length of any trip is determined by a boat's capacity to carry dog food -- $5 a pound here, if you can find it. And you can't find it.

At better than a pound of food a day, that's a lot on the way out as well. When we couldn't reach shore she reluctantly deposited her pootsies - poop Tootsie rolls - on the front deck.

In Florida, we had our shakedown cruises in the St. Lucie canal, which has locks to control the water. People always gather to watch the boats inside the lock raise or lower 18 feet.

Inevitably Raisin would pick this time - with a big audience - to deposit a big stinky gift on the bow. Maybe it was the inevitable applause.

I dove between the jumbled sail bags and managed to lift the cushion and reach into the big storage locker. I grab a hard, lumpy corner. Purina, for sure! I yanked and a 40-pound dog food bag toppled onto the floor. That'll work, right there, I thought. No need to drag it anywhere now.

I looked outside. The black line was as wide as a bandaid now and I could see the charcoal towering clouds roiling upwards from 40,000 feet. The ocean below was more white than black, wave tops shearing off from the wind.

# ISLAND

# CHAPTER 12

# August 6,  early evening

"We're stripped for action, kid," I tell Raisin.

"Lead the way. Steak, rare, baked potato with butter, Cesar salad. Ice cream. Yes, ice cream. Lots of ice cream. Can you do that?"

The long tail whips from side to side in anticipation of leftovers. Good luck, I think. I may never see another steak.

"You! Your purina days are over. From now on we're both on a seafood diet -- if we see food, we eat it. Ha ha." Her golden eyes glisten up at me.

As I scramble to the very top of the bluff, maneuvering becomes even more difficult.

I clamber over fallen trees and broken limbs, all covered with steaming mush left by nature's biggest blender.

I wonder if I can eat this stuff. Boil it up maybe into a soup if I can find enough dry twigs to make a fire. If I had some matches or a lighter.  If I had a pot to boil it in. "If we had some eggs, we could have some eggs and bacon, if we had some bacon," my mother used to say.

Water doesn't worry me. I'm parched, but I have a plan.

There's no use looking yet, until the wind subsides a little more, but there are bound to be containers washed up inland that hold fresh rainwater. If not yet, then I'll make sure that buckets fill with the next rain. Squalls are bound to follow.I glance at the sky. The clouds are still whipping by, white and fluffy. No rain there.

I may have to try Plan B. In Plan B I simply investigate every water-filled crevice and container I happen on.

At worst, they'll have brackish water from the salt spray everywhere and I may taste one or two things I'd rather not think about.

At best, I'll find a reasonably clean pail that landed upright and filled up with some of that torrential rain, and didn't get too much junk or sand or dead things. Raisin is less choosy.

Dirty is irrelevant. Brackish no problem at all. No doubt about it, food is going to be the biggy.

# STORM

# CHAPTER 13

# August 1, evening

We clambered below, not knowing what to expect.

Jim had barely made it into the cockpit when the full force of the wind and rain reached us. The temperature, already chill, collapsed. The rigging's moan climbed in pitch to a shrill note I'd never heard, like terrified monkeys.

Jim dropped behind the protection of the pilothouse just as a gust snapped the boat against her lines so hard we thought she was airborne. That gust, over 70, carried rain so driving it would have peeled skin if we'd exposed ourselves to it. The storm's coal-black clouds enveloped us, and submerged us in a living hell of liquid fury.

We scrambled to get inside. I backed through the door into the pilot house, grasping at the table for balance as Jim burst in in a blaze of lightning and liquefied air. The sound of the rippling crack momentarily overcame the rigging's scream.

Water streamed around the door as Jim yanked it shut. I grabbed a piece of line to tie it closed. My wet fingers trembled as I snugged the line and looped it through the handle. This will never do, I thought. We'll never live through this.

In the seconds it took to secure the line holding the door, the driving rain swamped the pilothouse. Water cascaded around the door and down the insides of the darkened windows.

Jim leaned against the navigation table and pitched his sodden rain-gear onto the dry side of the dinette. He finger combed his streaming hair out of his eyes and started to unclasp the safety harness he wore, designed to inflate if it's submerged, then thought better of it and snugged it tighter instead.

Out of habit, he stood on the steps leading to the main salon and gazed blindly at the plywood covering the center window.

Behind him, I was hanging on to the table for balance, wondering how to slow the water cascading through every crack.

My legs were spread and I leaned forward across the table, grasping with elbows and hands to stay upright. The table base, two inches of stainless steel, was screwed and glued to the floor, the best handhold in the boat.

Dry? You're worried about dry? Worry about floating, about surviving for God's sake, I said to myself. Wet can be fixed. Dead can't. The inner me shouted at the outer me. When I could move, I shoved the towels as best I could in the appropriate puddles and took stock. I could barely see. The sky was dark as pitch, even though it was't even suppertime.

The sky lit like noon with massive lightning strikes all around. The noise of the wind in the rigging and the electric shocks of lightning were unnerving. I tried not to succumb to terror.

# ISLAND

# CHAPTER 14

# August 7, afternoon

From the crest of the craggy bluff, or as near to it as I can get, I survey much of what remains of the island, the shape of the tiniest sliver of a new moon, substantially higher at one end — where I'm standing — than at the other where the beach dwindles to an extended sandbar.

A half-mile off the sandbar, a smaller, more rugged island stands looking just as wilted and torn.  Even with the dropping tide, little land is exposed, just the higher spots.

The inland scrub forest of the larger island is flooded, naked trees emerging from swampy muck like something out of Grimm's Fairy Tales.

Beyond the bluff and across another tidal cut is a third small island. In some ways, it's more picturesque than the larger one we thought of as "our island" because it was the one on the charts, and it had old signs of habitation -- a chickee hut in poor repair and several coral rock fireplaces.

After a couple of exploratory visits, we spent little time there because it was further from the anchored boat and the sand shallows extended a huge distance.

The beach at low tide was beyond words, acres of flawless pink sugar. But it meant a long walk in from the Whaler, and we were lazy. What can I say?

At least this little survey tells me I'm still "at home," I think. I must have washed overboard and been carried by the surge onto the beach. But where's the boat? Why isn't Jim out looking for me? Where is he?

I lean back against a broken limb. Jesus, I'm beat. I'm thirsty, I'm starved and every inch of me, inside and out, is sore. In those Dirk Pitt books, nature beats him to a pulp and he gets up swinging. I couldn't swing at a gnat.

"Raisin! We're going back down. Come on!" She ducks under a tangle of branches and reappears 20 feet down the slope. "Ah, the joys of being two feet tall. Wait up. Just like Jimmy Buffett said, My back aches, my feet stink and I'm goin' home to Jesus! Well, maybe not quite yet."

The sun is lower in the sky by the time I retrieve my rain gear and sweat shirt, and the tide is dropping fast. By the time I reach the bottom, at least 15 feet of beach shows where it had been a mucky five-foot swamp.

Steaming piles of brown goo marked the high water line. It looks like every conceivable bit of floating debris on the planet has been nestled in its grasp -- plastic bottles of every size, shape and description, jar lids, glass bottles, jugs, cans, styrofoam floats, polypropylene line in every color and size. I'm stunned, but I realize I shouldn't be. I've seen enough damage from other storms to have an inkling of what to expect.

I sit on the strand of sand near the leafy nest that had saved me. I burrow in so I can rest my back, and Raisin flops next to me with her chin in my lap. "Enough play," she seems to be telling me. "Let's go home."

Fine by me. Lead the way, I think. Slowly, the memories of the terrible storm, 'Yes, Mr. Jones, the worst experience of my life,' are coming back to me.

# STORM

# CHAPTER 15

# August 2, wee hours

A single 12-volt light cut the gloom of the plywood-shrouded cabin. It was light enough to locate a screwdriver, and to see the fear in each other's faces, but that was it.

Spare line buried the aft dinette seat, no doubt damp and salty by now.

The awning and its poles stretched from the door to extend over the steps into the main salon. Piled on top of the awning on the port side were the tools we'd used getting ready. Carelessly abandoned or close by in readiness? I wondered.

It was the spot where Jim dumped nearly all of his tools, rather than put them away.

It was one of the festering sore spots of our relationship, the Chinese water torture of surviving together in a confined space. He dumped. I sorted and put away.

When he asked where something was, I always knew. If, in a snit, I declined and they piled up to the point where he put them away, he merely hid them out of sight and promptly forgot where.

Then my aggravation was even greater, because I inevitably ended up with the task of finding the desperately needed implement in the middle of a project.

On top of the awning was my life-saving gear, what I acknowledged in my compulsion as my man-overboard bag, pared down in the last few months to a weight that could actually be lifted.

It contained the crazy things suggested by people who had been lost at sea for long stretches, then rescued — a deck of plastic cards, a few pounds of uncooked rice, fish hooks by the hundred. A dictionary. A Bible. Whistles. Bells. Lights. Lots of odd things assembled over years of worrying about being a thousand miles from nowhere with just that bag.

Jim was disgusted with it, claimed it was still too heavy to heft if we were in such rough conditions.

It was lighter than the bag I had when I had my own boat, I'd tell him. "Don't worry. If it comes to that, I'll heft the goddam thing. Believe me."  I needed to inventory the bag. Later.

On top of the bag, our two very good life jackets, two floating flashlights, a red plastic horn too big to fit in the bag, a sheet of indestructible rust-colored vinyl I'd been toting around for 10 years, with slices missing from covering the windows, two spare rain jackets and two not-too-wet sweatshirts.

Raisin was still curled up under the dinette table. She didn't appear to be on top of anything important for a change.

On the forward dinette seat, Jim's sodden rain jacket and hat lay on top of the two furry blankets I'd pulled out for us to bundle up in. More likely they'd be used for mopping up.  They already were.

# ISLAND

# CHAPTER 16

# August 6, late afternoon

My aching back demands I move away from the comfy rock. I scrape the sticky tendrils of hair out of my eyes and wipe more sand off my face, then pull at Raisin's brown floppy ears. She loves it, especially when I dig my fingers deep into their roots and rub hard. She scrunches all 70 pounds to push back on my fingers. She almost purrs.

"Break time's over, kid. Up and at 'em. Food and shelter, whaddya say?"

As I creak to my knees and struggle to stand, Raisin rolls over, kicking her legs and wriggling her bony back in the soft sand. Snake practice. Which reminds me, looking at the gooey mess that was most of the island, thank goodness there are no poisonous snakes in the Bahamas.

If this were Florida, we'd probably both be dead from water moccasins and rattlers. I remember after one storm seeing a water moccasin nearly as long as the boat zigzagging through the water. Thank God for small favors. As it is, all I have to worry about is drowned curlytails. Maybe they can swim. Maybe I can cook one!

Raisin trots off along the ever-widening beach. I glance at the sky. It must be close to 5 or 6 by now, I judge. Nearing low tide. I glance back at the bluffs and judge low tide to be at least three feet higher than the normal high. That means a lot less beach when the water started rising again.

I need a dry, safe spot for the night. I need to find Jim. And the boat.

They must be ok, how could they not be? I'm fine. Fine being relative. And I have to find food.

What could there possibly be, short of a windfall of plastic-wrapped sandwiches dropping from the sky?

I actually break a smile, remembering that crazy movie about the falling meatballs. No such luck. If I find a can of something blown in from somewhere, I can't open it.

My itchy, hazy eyes probe the high water line along the dune. Just ahead of Raisin, a hump of smooth green peeps through the debris.

"Halleluya, Raisin! Lookee there, kid!" I shout with glee.

Raisin looks at my pointing finger, tail rigid, ears on full alert. "Get the coco. Where's the coco?"

She bounds over the dune, madly looking left and right for her favorite beach toy.

Mature brown-husked coconuts take her about five minutes to shred down to a clean nut. The nut becomes a combination soccer ball and float toy, a focus of intense yapping excitement that occupies her for hours.

A green coconut, like the one I'd spotted, takes longer to husk and isn't as much fun, because the nut inside is more fragile. But she'd settle, and so will I.

The trick will be diverting her attention so I can grab the nut before she breaks it and the milk pours out. I can drink the milk and scrape the mushy meat out with my fingernails.

Even one nut will provide a filling meal if I get it all. Raisin can have a few bites but coconuts make her sick.

# STORM

## CHAPTER 17

## August 2, wee hours

I couldn't believe it. I was getting seasick, something I'd never even considered.

Only an hour had passed from when we barred the door. The main cabin floor had three inches of water over it already and the few things I hadn't put away or had lodged on the settee were slamming back and forth into the sparkling mahogany drawers below the seat.

One cabinet had burst open and cans of soup and other staples rolled and rolled and rolled, trapped between and bouncing over those effing awning poles.

I could feel that last hunk of bread and butter rising perilously in my throat and the telltale rush of saliva… think about something else, anything else! Think about a summer day exploring for perfect shells..

No way! Those goddam poles! I thought. The stainless fittings gouging again and again into the glistening wood. I gritted my teeth and tried not to scream. But the anger was overcoming my urge to upchuck.

My poor boat! Poor me! The noise was beyond horrific. A sound louder than a lifting jet screamed in rigging shrieking for mercy.

The motion of the boat was a thousand times more terrifying than the worst carnival ride I'd ever been on. She would dance forward on the anchor line, then race back to stop like a car crashing into a bridge.

In the space of 30 seconds, I would be nearly upright on my seat, then a deadly pause like the top of a roller coaster, and the motion reversed. At the same time, the boat pitched into the rollers, lifting, lifting, pointing at the sky, then diving over the crests straight down. A giant Mixmaster.

My fingers were raw from grasping the edge of the table and my legs shuddered with tension cramps. I was shaking with fear and cold. If God had made a hell, this was it.

Dings in the finish of the carefully varnished wood was the least of my worries. Raisin seemed the only calm one, jammed up against the hull, still under the table. She was a tight ball, curled like a snake with her head jammed into her tummy and legs tight beneath her.

Jim was laid out on his belly on the floor of the main salon, what floor there was, oily water sloshing over him with the movement. He had on his life jacket and was gripping a float from the Whaler. A wool knitted watchman's hat covered his ears and his balding head. His body rocked back and forth, trapped between the man overboard bag and the galley half-wall.

The mass of poles, awning, detritus rocked with him. Every minute or two he would emit a low moan, almost too low to hear over the noise of the storm but clear enough to detect a mind sliding into oblivion.

# ISLAND

# CHAPTER 18

# August 7, morning

Raisin finds a green husk and yelps with glee as her head bobs to push it out of its hiding place. It was her habit to play soccer for a bit before getting down to the business of husking, so I watch her roll the nut to the edge of the water and let it float a few feet away.

She pounces like it's a wild thing and sinks her teeth into the diamond-hard husk, burying her face in the water while she secures her grip. Hooray for those pit bull teeth, I think. That's breakfast in there, or at least a snack.

She gnashes those teeth and pulls away a few scraps of green, showing the thick white strands beneath. Again and again she attacks the husk, yapping in her anticipation of the prize inside. It's lots better than any Crackerjack toy.

She's not as fast as a Bahamian with a razor sharp machete, but no ordinary human can clear a green coconut in the 15 minutes it takes her. At the end she's exhausted and panting, proudly nosing the pale, hairy nut along the beach. I let her have her fun for another minute while I scout for a big, loose rock. I really want one that's sharp or has a point.

Finally a solitary chunk of moon rock glistens at me.

Just the job, I think. Now to get the coconut back.

"Raisin!" I call. " Raisin! Where's the coco?" She grasps it in her jaws and comes prancing towards me. "What a good girl! Thank you!"

That's her cue, a hard-learned lesson to let go of whatever she's holding - a shoe, a precious piece of mahogany trim, a bunny. She drops her prize at my feet and looks stricken with grief. Good girl! I rub her ears and pick it up.

"Let's find another coco! Where's the coco?" Raisin spins like a top and zigzags away along the beach. Another hunt!

I continue toward the rocks, stepping over the layers of detritus the storm had left. Nothing useful yet, I think.

Nothing plastic appeared in one piece, but there are thousands of bits of margarine containers, cracked water bottles and milk jugs, shards of red gas cans, pieces of tarp, miles of tangled polypropylene line, fishing line, the occasional colorful float. Just one container, I wish. Just one with four sides and a bottom with no holes. I'll settle for a bottle, even a small one. But no cracks. Impossible.

I reach the rocks, cradling the coconut and my rock. I need to find a hollow the right size to hold the nut steady. Or I need a brave third hand. Right! That's not in the cards, is it?

I have to make this work.

The first trick is to pierce the three soft spots at the top of the nut. I'll settle for two — one to let the milk out and the other to let the air in. I'd done it with an electric drill a few times, and once with a hammer and a big nail.

Show-off tough guys will slam the thing down onto a nail or screw and pierce it that way, but they lose a lot of milk. And their aim has to be perfect or the hard husk just laughs at the nail and bends it.

So I'm looking for a nice holder and there it is. A little water-filled indentation with some arms sticking up. I'll need to be careful.

One of those sharp bastards would rip my hand open in a New York second. I glance around   for Raisin. She's still exploring, this time up to her chest in the water. The chop is still fierce with wind now out of the south.

I nestle the coconut into the hollow and eye the rock in my hand. Maybe five pounds and the size of a big tomato can but more pear shaped and a little scary to hold because of its sharp edges. One side has a nice point that I hope is big enough to do the deed. I turn the rock over and explore one eye of the coconut. Lookin' good! I think. I twist the point into the nut a few times and grind a small divot into one eye, then lift the rock about a foot and pray my aim is true.

# STORM
# CHAPTER 19
# Aug. 2, morning

It had been nine hours. Nine hours of ceaseless violent motion. Nine hours of deafening, terrifying noise. Nine hours watching the water level creep up the walls of the main cabin, knowing it was nearing the air intake for the diesel engine below us. Nine hours of watching foot-high waves take over the inside of this boat, the love of my life. Nine hours amassing bruises on top of bruises and praying my hands wouldn't lose their grip.

Jim had collapsed. He had moved to the higher pilot house floor, but still rolled from side to side, bashing his head and his legs. His only protection was the life jacket sodden with rain and salt water streaming through the door and the sides of the windows. His pitiful moan had stopped.

I knew he was still conscious because his hands grasped the solid step in front of the door. Its top had long since disappeared somewhere below, but the inch-thick base was glued and screwed to a heavy beam. That step held an array of small hand tools - screwdrivers, pliers, clamps — all now awash in oily water.

But finally, after nine hours, I could discern a softening of the motion, a slightly lower tone in the screaming rigging. We had gone through the worst.

Anything that was going to break was broken. Anything that would survive already had.  My precious brass oil lamps still clung to the bulkheads. Even the glass chimneys stayed on. A miracle!

My prized watercolor of a storm-ravaged boat was mounted high enough on the bulkhead next to the settee that it got only occasional splashes.

 But the cushions, the supplies,, all of the books and charts, mingled in the oily stew stirring on the floor of the main cabin. Every cabinet, even those taped and tied shut, had exploded from the pressure

# ISLAND
# CHAPTER 20
# August 7, morning

Wham! With both hands I smash the pointy rock onto the top of the coconut. I miss the spot. Damn. Again! Wham!

This time my aim is truer, and a tiny crack ventures out from the top of the nut. I needed to go deeper, so I jam the point into the eye and push and wriggle it as hard as I can with both hands.

The holder is perfect. Come on! Get in there! I exhort the rock.

Another big slam and the nut shows a darker streak along the crack. Milk! I lick it to make sure and taste that familiar sweetness. There won't be much, I think, too green. But maybe that's better.

Sure enough, with the next whack, the crack widens and a sliver of the outside crust crumbles away. My finger invades the hole and my broken nail snags a taste of the soft meat inside. Delicious! Even with the sand coating my fingers.

Raisin's incredible nose alerts her and she raises her head to get a better sniff. On she comes at a run. I tap the nut once more and it splits into two jagged pieces, two misshapen bowls coated with coconut the consistency of a ripe banana. Yum! Raisin arrives as I scrape a second finger full.

"Here, a treat," I stick my hand out and she laps it like ice cream. "That's it. More later. Go find another one!" Reluctantly, she bounds back along the beach, eyes peeled for that special shade of green. I settle down for my first food in… in when? It was a blank.

# STORM

# CHAPTER 23

# August 2, afternoon.

The wind and rain had finally let up to the level of an ordinary torrential storm. We could finally hear the noise of the ocean waves crashing up against the dunes and rocks on the exposed side of the island.

Exposed? I laughed to myself. Like we weren't exposed! A hundred plus miles of shallow bay to our southwest, twice that in the other direction, and this little boomerang of sand 30 feet high and maybe a mile wide, three miles long, tops. A few hundred yards of mangroves, sea grape, pines and sand between us and England.

Next stop if we miss the Bahamas! We'd utter the mantra every time we left Florida. The Gulf Stream was an unforgiving mistress, marching steadily northeast at a couple of knots, tough for a four-knot sailboat to sail against.

Waves in the bay had dropped from at least six feet to three, leaving the heavy boat feeling relatively steady. I inched my way across the sodden dinette cushion and glanced at Jim, still clutching the step base.

He seemed asleep. I put one foot in the space between him and the dinette, then stood, straddling his prone body, to view the wreckage below. I grasped the bronze handrails and looked down the steps into the main salon and v-berth.

Oh my god… a moan escaped me. Worse than I thought. So much worse. All that work. All that money… gone. Just gone. We're done. Done.

I looked at the filthy water roiling nearly two feet above the floor, level with the settee cushions. Halfway up the engine. Black oil on every surface, thrown by the waves. The smell. Oh my god. The engine…

I turned to face the door. The wind and rain were even less. With two careful steps past Jim I reached the door and started untying the line lashing the handle to the bulkhead.

Rain still seeped in but it didn't matter any more. I folded the door and pushed it open. Miraculously, the mizzen boom was still in place.

I turned to look at the main mast. Cracked. I could see a huge split lengthwise, probably from the weight of the thrashing boom, lashed against the mizzen mast. It was still hooked at both ends, but the crack reached halfway up. It was firewood.

I turned to look for the Whaler. Nothing, a distant memory, washed out to sea or what? They never sink, that's true, but they'll fill to the gunnels and become invisible. I knew that for a fact.

# MAIDEN VOYAGE
## CHAPTER 22

The year before, we'd had our maiden voyage in the boat we had slaved over for what felt like an eternity. Of all our "trips from hell" this one took the cake. Until now, I thought.

This one clearly takes first prize.

We had lost the engine in Marsh Harbour. Our return had been delayed because I'd broken a molar and had to wait for a crown. Then I cracked a bone in my wrist and couldn't even pull on a bathing suit or stir a pot of soup without screaming in pain.

So we stayed put and finally headed west in early November, just in time to be wary of the northers and what those winds did to the Gulf Stream - the ocean would look like badly mashed potatoes with 10 foot waves popping up every which way. No fun at all.

But we had to get back. We were broke. Jim's credit card had expired. And we needed fuel and water.

Jim could get some cash from the bank in Freeport. That meant taking a bus from West End. Then we could buy gas for the Whaler, fresh water, diesel for Wham B'Ama.

But when departure day arrived, we had just fired up the engine when it emitted an enormous clunk and stopped cold.

Not a wheeze, not a sputter, just a sound like a sledgehammer hitting solid iron. Then nothing. Very bad. We knew it. We didn't even speak. We each took to our separate corners and sat in silence. All day.

And yes, it's a sailboat, but sailboats move with their engine nearly all the time. The engine powers the batteries that run the lights, the navigation system, the autopilot, the fresh water pump, the fridge. The bilge pumps!

The complications of no engine are endless. Getting home just under sail, not just uncomfortable but nearly impossible.

At best, we'd have to tow Wham B'Ama with the Whaler and run our tiny emergency generator to power the basics. The conditions had to be perfect.

So we waited.

The next morning, we started rigging the Whaler to tow Wham B'Ama. We set up fenders to protect both boats from bumping each other and spring lines to keep the Whaler snugged up to the cockpit so Jim could climb in and out.

Although I could steer Wham B'Ama with the wheel, Jim would have to stay in the Whaler to control the outboard's speed.

As well as towing the boat, we had to run the small portable generator to keep the batteries up. We needed batteries for the radio to talk to other boats, the single-side-band radio for weather reports, running lights, the depth sounder and instruments, and — praise the lord — the autopilot.

Securing the generator in the cockpit so the cables reached the battery bank was tricky. The little generator, the size of a sewing machine, ended up on the seat, with the cables running through a gap in the bottom.

The tiny tank only held about two hours worth of gas, so we used some plastic tube to make a longer hose for the gas can nozzle and keep spillage to a minimum. It only went off while we slept. The sound pierced my head like a dentist's drill.

If it sputtered and stopped, pull-starting it was more than I could do, so Jim would have to stop the outboard, climb into Wham B'Ama, pull-start that motor, then clamber back down into the Whaler and start the outboard, all while we drifted in the wrong direction.

Once we were ready, the wind inevitably came from the direction we needed to go.

Then there was no wind.

Later, a norther was coming.

The wind was too strong.

We got nightly personalized forecasts from a ham operator in Germany. After a while, his accented voice became the sound I heard in my head.

But slowly, mile after mile, warning after warning, over weeks we inched our way past Manjack, where we had spent weeks exploring, Powell, where sailors hung mementoes in the Message Tree to show they'd been there, on past Cooperstown, where I had phoned my dad on his very last Father's Day.

# MAIDEN VOYAGE

## CHAPTER 23

Father's Day that year dawned gray and fierce in a summer already unique in its nasty personality. Jim and I had sailed to the Abacos in the northern Bahamas in April and spent the next two months dodging thunderstorms, squalls, waterspouts and blazing lightning storms. The approach of midsummer hadn't improved things.

Nevertheless, Father's Day signified a command performance for me. I had been warning Jim for days: "Don't forget, we need to be at a phone on Sunday."

Phones required serious advance planning for us. We spent most of our time anchored off one of the dozens of unpopulated islands on the northern side of Abaco Sound.

Our tentative plan was to head into Green Turtle Cay for some fresh veggies and Irish butter, and to call home. My dad was 79 that summer, in failing health that wasn't improved by his worry about his crazy firstborn's cruising life. He knew a gift was out of the question, but he would be crushed if I failed to wish him a Happy Father's Day by phone.

We had been holed up at Manjack Cay, a desert island in every sense of the word. Its boomerang shape offered enough protection for our heavy displacement Newporter 40 in all but the worst weather, and the island was so big it offered a marvelous variety of land and seascapes for exploring.

The vast curved beach on the anchorage side let us land our 13-foot Whaler with ease. We hung a marker in a tree so we could always find the path that led to a big protected bay on the ocean side.

At low tide, the pink beach was awash with hundreds of sand dollars and small shells. Raisin spent countless hours chasing baby sharks in the shallows. Other parts of the island offered expanses of moonrock, felled trees, birds, crabs and incredibly gin-clear water.

But one thing Manjack didn't have was a phone. A few days before Father's Day, I suggested we head for Green Turtle. The weather was lousy: windy from the wrong direction and nasty afternoon storms.

By Saturday, we were facing a 15-knot headwind, making for a sloppy and slow motorboat ride, so we decided to hold out for a promise of improved weather the next day. Wrong. It was worse. Lots worse. There was no way we could slog to Green Turtle in a day, even under power.

Cooperstown, however, was opposite us on what the locals call the "mainland," the barrier island hub of Great Abaco, a short five miles across Abaco Sound.

"I'll just take the Whaler over," I suggested at breakfast. Jim had been in a steadily deteriorating mood, right along with the weather.

I was game to run the Whaler, despite the fact that my right arm was in a splint, thanks to a nasty case of carpal tunnel. I could run it all right, but pull-starting the 20-horse Johnson outboard was excruciating, and climbing a ladder one-armed never failed to be an adventure. I was hoping Jim would volunteer to take me, eliminating the worst of my problems.

As he thought it over, we watched conditions in Abaco Sound deteriorate. Outside the protection of Powell's northern arm, we could see three-foot waves. Between the cereal and the second cup of coffee, the waves built and the wind started whipping off the tops.

"Let's just take the big boat over. We'll fuel up as well," Jim suggested. That sounded like the best of both worlds to me. A comfortable ride, and no spray-soaking. Little did I know.

In the couple hours it took us to up the well-embedded anchors and bounce our way over to Cooperstown, the wind had increased even more.

The high fuel dock at Cooperstown Shell is fully exposed to the seas, and the shore is rocky and steep, two strikes against us reaching shore. It was far too rough to bring 'Bama in to the fuel dock so we dropped the big CQR anchor and prayed it would hold in the scaled bottom.

By then, the waves had built to five feet and the Whaler bucked like a bronco on its tether next to the big boat, level with Wham B'Ama's deck on the crests and a full story down in the troughs. Jim leapt in first and started the outboard. I pocketed a $10 bill, snugged up my arm brace and tried to time my tumble into the Whaler… jump is far too kind a word.

By this time, 30-knot winds were blowing the crests off steep five-foot seas. It was all Jim could do to make headway the 100 yards to the Cooperstown dock and it was all I could do to hang on.

As we neared the dock, I needed to grab the ladder, secure the line from the boat and clamber the eight feet up to the dock. Sure.

I crouched in the bow, the painter - the line from the Whaler - in my bad right hand, reaching out with my left to grab the closest upright as soon as it came within reach.

We were performing a nightmarish ballet, desperately trying to coordinate the push of the engine with the surge and lift of the waves.  The little boat pirouetted in random directions.

The wind tried to blow us into the massive pilings, and the beam seas threatened to overturn the Whaler if we got sideways. The rocky shore was too close for comfort, and one wrong move would send us crashing.

Jim edged as close as he could. I grabbed the ramshackle ladder and missed. We surged back. I grabbed again.

The first rung of the ladder was at waist level when the Whaler crested. It was over my head in the trough. My right arm was all but useless, good only to hang the painter on. But conditions weren't improving. I had to try.

The Whaler surged and lifted, I grabbed the splintered upright, wrapped my good left arm around and tried to find support as the Whaler flew away under my feet. Jim madly reversed the motor and swerved to keep from crashing into the dock.

For one split second, I thought I had it. For the tiniest blink of an eye, I was weightless, had the ladder in one arm and thought I'd made it.

Then gravity took over. My left arm couldn't support all my weight, I couldn't reach the lowest rung of the ladder and I fell backwards in slow motion into the churning water as the Whaler bucked away from the dock.

In automatic response, I clenched my eyes shut to protect my contact lenses as I dropped and the seas closed over my head. The propeller missed me by inches.

Jim circled to pick me up and I back paddled away from the heaving boat inches away from me. I shouted that I would swim for it.

It was deep almost to the bank, where I encountered countless years of harvested conchs, like slimy spiked bowling balls. I struggled to my knees, grasping at the slick rocklike conch shells for support and struggled out of the water and slowly up the steep bank.

Sodden, stinking and scratched from the conchs, I walked into the closet-sized Cooperstown Shell office at the base of the long, high dock.

The Bahamian man sitting at the cluttered desk simply raised his eyebrows at my appearance. A smile haunted his eyes. It would have been impolite to laugh outright. Bahamians are very polite.

"Good afternoon," he said.

"Good afternoon. I fell in," I offered, although my appearance spoke for itself. "Can you help me? I'm looking for a phone."

He directed me down the only street and past some bright but tattered homes cluttered with dark, playful children and scrawny dogs. The children waved and smiled as I walked by, my cotton dress drying quickly in the brisk wind.

The phone beckoned. I prayed it had all its parts. Many public phones were missing key pieces -- the handset, a cord, the coin box. This one, like most, was filthy and the protective plastic shell was cracked. It had a credit card slot instead of a coin box -- one of the newfangled phones the Bahamian Telephone Company was using to replace the old-fashioned coin phones. I lifted the handset and discovered a nasty secret -- no dial tone. No coin box. No way to call an operator. No way to dial out.

I returned to the Shell office to inquire about another phone, one I could use to call collect.

"Sorry miss, 'dat de only phone. You hab to have de phone card."

"Where do I do that?" I asked.

"At de Batelco office, miss. Dat de only place. They not open today. Anyway, they not here. They in Treasure."

"But today is Sunday. I have to make this call today to my father," I said. "Today is Father's Day, and I have to call today. I can't wait."

"Sorry miss, dat de only phone," he said.

My heart sank. I knew what I was going through to make this call, but I knew that my dad's perspective was completely different. If I failed to call on Father's Day, he would think I was busy basking on some sunny shore and had simply forgotten. He wouldn't be angry. He would be terribly hurt.

"Isn't there anywhere in town I can buy a phone card today?" I asked Mr. Shell. "Do you know anyone who has a card they would let me buy?"

"The store don't have dem, miss," he said. "But de store not open anyway. It bein' Sunday. On'y Batelco.

"I hab an old one but it on'y have a copple dollah left on it. It wouldn't he'p you."

"It would, it would," I begged. "If I can just get through long enough to say hello, that's all I need. He'll understand. I just need time to say a few words. Can I buy your card? Please?"

I fumbled for the crumpled, sodden bill in the depths of my pocket.

"Here. Here's $10 for your card. Won't you sell it to me for that? Please? I don't care how much time is left." He fingered the dripping bill.

"I hab it at home. I b to see how much is on it. You wait here."

He unraveled his long limbs from the tattered chair and walked out the door. "I be right back. You wait here," he said, firing up a rusted Chevy whose muffler was a distant memory.

Minutes passed. I watched 'Bama straining against her anchor chain, pitching madly in the short, steep chop of the sound. The sky was darkening. Rain would come soon.

"Good Lord," I thought. "I'll be sleeping here if this keeps up. I'll never get back onto the boat, even if I have a prayer of making it into the Whaler."

Jim had managed to tie the Whaler off to the big dock, and was serenely riding it out in the slight protection offered by the massive pilings. The only ladder -- source of my ill-timed swim -- was on the other side. He was in for an adventure to pick me up, as well.

Finally, I heard a rumble as my newfound friend returned. He had a smile for me at last.

"Here you go, miss," he said. "I checked it. It got $1.80 left. I fill bad takin' your money for just dat li'l bit. I don't tink it will do you no good."

I assured him I was willing to take the risk. I gave him the $10 and shook his hand. "Thank you. Thank you so much," I said. "I know it's silly, but it's really important."

I walked back up the street clutching my treasure and slid it slowly into the slot. A dial tone! I quickly pressed the familiar buttons and waited while the prehistoric phone system clicked its way into the 20th century and reached out to touch Arizona.

"Hello?" The voice was gruff with age and weariness.

"HI!" I shouted. "Happy Father's Day! I can only talk for a minute -- long story."

"Ahh, well, thank you."

I could hear his sigh of relief. His daughter, floating somewhere on the seven seas, was still in this life. I was living a dream he had had in his younger years, but never fulfilled. I may be nearing 50, but I would always be his little girl.

"So, are you having a nice day? Enjoying the sun? Catching some fish?"

"Oh yes," I said. "We're having a marvelous time. Just a bit of trouble getting to a phone, but I'll tell you all about it later… you have a marvelous day today. I just wanted to say I love you and Happy Father's Day."

I hung up and turned to face my struggle back aboard Wham B'Ama, soaked, exhausted, but grateful I had managed the call despite the obstacles.

It was my dad's last Father's Day. He died the following spring, just four months short of his 80th birthday.

# STORM

# CHAPTER 26

# August 2, early evening

The relative quiet in the middle of the storm was brief, maybe a half hour of bits of blue sky and grey scudding clouds. The eye. Not quite centered over us, but close enough. This beast is headed for the Carolinas, I thought. Maybe Georgia if it veers west.

Nobody even cares where it is right now. We're just in the middle of some spaghetti lines on the Weather Channel. These islands aren't even specks on the maps.

I climbed out of the cockpit and onto the deck.

Raisin had dislodged herself from under the table and stayed at my heels, jamming her head into my elbow for an ear rub.

The rigging holding up the masts looked and felt solid, but that cracked mast was bad.

The mast went through the deck and was seated on the keel, below the main cabin floor.

If the mast broke apart or started to fall, it could rip out the deck, even the side of the cabin. If it started to swing around, that would be the end of everything.

There was nothing I or anyone could do. If we got through the back of the storm, maybe we could strap it together long enough to get somewhere. Or not.

The tiny staysail boom was right where I'd left it, snugged up to the main mast and clamped down hard on the forward hatch. Solid. Nice. Raisin had scampered up behind me. I knew she wanted to reach land to pee, but that wasn't in the cards.

"It's ok, girl, it's ok. You can pee here." She tossed me a sorrowful look and dutifully squatted.

I know just how she feels, I thought, and pulled my bathing suit aside to join her. There was so much water on the deck and more coming, I knew nature would take care of the rinsing.

The anchor lines looked worn and the chafing gear was a twisted mess, but the anchors must be close to the earth's inner core by now, I thought. They'll be a bear to lift. The least of our worries.

I checked the sky and saw the darkening eye wall edging closer. I needed to get back below and find something to eat and drink before it hit. The back side is always worse, and we were much more exposed when the wind switched.

The tiny island had offered a little protection, but now we would have the full strength of the storm and nothing to hide behind when it hit.

I stepped back into the pilot house where Jim was still on the floor, but now on his back with his arms covering his face.

"Bad," I told him. "Really really bad. But the anchors held. Maybe we'll make it." He lowered an elbow and peered with one eye, then rolled onto his stomach. Silence. That was Jim.  In the face of disaster, full retreat.

I wondered yet again what kind of soldier he'd been in Vietnam. A medic, I knew, but when the gunfire came, did he keep going or make up a reason to dive into a bunker?

I stepped into the watery mess of the main salon and grabbed an oil-coated bottle of root beer floating next to the settee.

I found two nearby cans, the labels washed off, and a jar of strawberry jam. That would have to do, I thought.

Can opener? Beyond a miracle, the galley drawer that always stuck was still stuck. One can opener coming up! Yes!

I returned to the pilot house with my spoils and stuffed them behind a cushion in the dinette corner and retied the door. I pushed the sodden towels and rags into the spaces and grabbed the big yellow flashlight that had been rolling around for hours.

A bit of light had brightened the gloom during the first half of the storm, but night was falling and the flashlight might ease the terrors I knew were coming.

Minutes later, wedged in my corner, the wind careening out of the southwest knocked Wham B'Ama all the way over onto her side.

The only thing saving us from filling up with water then and there was the two-foot wide deck, but the main cabin windows in the widest part of the boat took a bad beating and started gushing saltwater before her heavy keel took over and pulled us back from the brink.

Solid rain blasted us like a waterfall and we may as well have been under the sea as on top of it. The noise again was deafening and Wham B'Ama spun on her anchors to face what was coming.

# MAIDEN VOYAGE
## CHAPTER 25

After Cooperstown and its acres of conch shells came Foxtown, where we were warned not to stop. Drug runners. Common knowledge.

So many memories. That's where we saw the hammerhead! Over there, the cove where we dragged and had to pull the anchor at 3 a.m. There! Where I dove for that huge triton!

On to Grand Cay, then the long hop to West End and the 60 open ocean miles to Florida.

Anywhere in Florida. Just Florida. As long as we could head west, we'd reach something.

Grand Cay is home to the Bahamians who keep up Walker's Cay, the exclusive country club island catering to sport fishermen next door.

Grand has a tiny church with six pews and two dozen welcoming smiles. The three-hour Sunday sermons are peppered with hymns like "Jesus Loves Me," and questions from the preacher about ailing moms and distant friends.

The women parade their finest dresses and their hats are a sight to behold.. Stand aside, Kentucky Derby, you ain't seen nothin' like this! It was a religious experience for sure.

Grand also has a tiny general store the size of a walk-in closet. The rotund, happy proprietor sits on a rickety chair with her youngest snuggled on her lap. She sells single eggs, cereal by the cupful and Oreo cookies by the "stick," one cellophane-wrapped section of cookies from a larger box.

I splurged on a stick of Oreos. The rest of the cash - except $5 for the West End bus - went for gas for the Whaler.

If Jim got to the bank and couldn't cash a check, he wouldn't even have the money to get back to the boat, let alone pay for water, more gas, and the dock where I would wait with Wham B'Ama.

Nearly all of the trip from Marsh Harbour had been under power from the Whaler. Most days we lashed the small boat alongside and Jim steered, but sometimes as a break from the noise, he'd rig a tow line and go in front.

Either way, holding a straight course was near impossible and we spent as much time correcting our path as moving in the right direction. I stayed at the wheel in Wham B'Ama, steering as well, and keeping an eye on the compass. The portable generator puttered away on the cockpit seat.

# MAIDEN VOYAGE
## CHAPTER 26

On this day, the worst day of that Trip from Hell, we had left the protection of Grand for West End. The wind was barely a breath and the water was like a mirror. Jim raised the mainsail in hopes of a tiny assist before he settled into the Whaler for another brutal day. He paid out 70 feet of line and eased Wham B'Ama toward the channel.

The sail flapped and hung like dirty laundry for hours as we inched through glassy water. Eight feet below, starfish stretched their arms and conchs and helmets paraded their colors.

Then in the distance I spotted tiny ripples in the water, an old habit from my racing days when ripples signaled wind and better speed.

I felt a breath of air on my neck and the main fluttered. Jim hadn't noticed. The tow line slackened as the main seized a puff of air and gained some shape. The big boat started to close the gap on the Whaler.

I ran forward and yelled, "Do you want me to drop the sail?"

By then, Wham B'Ama was just 20 feet behind the Whaler. Jim still had his hand on the outboard's tiller and steered to the right of the big boat as she edged closer to him. He ran the engine up and gained a few feet but then fell back again.

"No, it's good. It's fine!" He shouted back. I reached the mast and asked again. "Are you sure?" He nodded hard with that look. 'Me, man! Me know best!' I could see the determination in his face as he pushed the Johnson to its limit.

In the seconds it took me to reach the cockpit, the bow of the Whaler had dropped even with the back of the big boat. The breeze quickened again and the mainsail filled.

The towline was nowhere to be seen, then in a flash the half-inch line snapped tight, the Whaler spun around so it was being towed backwards and water started rushing over the transom, swamping the motor and filling the boat.

Jim can't swim. He always wore a life belt.

"Cut the line! Cut the line!" I screamed as I leapt up onto the cabin and reached the mast. I unwrapped the halyard and clawed the huge mainsail down into a heap to slow the big boat.

I turned to see Jim dancing backwards on the Whaler seats as the stern fully submerged and water washed all the way to the bow.

Jim looked like a ballerina, bald, in tiny red speedos, on tiptoe and terror-stricken as he jumped from seat to seat away from the cascading water.

The stern and motor were fully submerged and the bow showed only a few inches. Jim dropped to his knees and managed to release the towline. Only the black rub rail and the top of the outboard showed above the waves.

Propelled by her own weight, Wham B'Ama traveled another 100 yards before I managed to set the anchor and stop the big boat.

The Whaler was fully awash, the Johnson outboard swamped. The gas tank was floating off to one side, held only by the fuel line. Everything inside the Whaler was gone, including the bailing bucket and the paddle. Jim couldn't swim and I couldn't move the big boat nearer to him.

# ISLAND

# CHAPTER 27

## August 7, afternoon

I'm facing the empty bay, squinting in the bright sun. Invisible. Not just the Whaler, I think, staring at sections of the water in a sequence, like looking for distant lights at night. There is not a sign of Wham B'Ama, or of Jim, or of any life but me and Raisin.

I'm relishing the soft coconut. Too much and I'll have the runs, like Whatshisname who survived the plane crash in that movie. But in this heat, it will spoil in a couple of hours. Ok. Half now, half in an hour. After I check the other side of the island.

"Come on Raisin!" I yell and she bounces through the waves to my side. We clamber back up the dune and slide down again to the ocean side.

So much plastic, nets, pieces of wood and junk had blown ashore, the oceanside beach is almost impassable. Not for Raisin. She picks her way through and I follow her route for 100 yards.

But it's a crazy task, and I call her to come back with me to the bay side. The tide is on the rise, the sun peeking through the flying clouds is getting low, and I'm worried about finding any protection before it gets too dark to see.

The wind has dropped to a bearable 15 to 20 miles an hour but the cloudy sky won't give us a moon. I can only hope the clouds might drop a little fresh water.

I dig my foul weather jacket out of its hidey hole and wish it wasn't still damp with salt water. It will never dry. Like my shorts, or sweatshirt, or bathing suit.

Some wardrobe, salt-soaked, sand crusted, stinking of oil and sweat. Nice. Not like those magazine shots of bikini-clad hotties tanning on a snow-white deck with their Cosmos and their boy-toys and whitewashed Mediterranean houses in the background. What a laugh!

I put my now-empty coconut husk to work and dig out a space near the top of the dune and lay out my jacket. The seaweed looks and feels too nasty for a bed and I decide I'd rather suffer the hard than the stink. I gather some big sea grape leaves to make a bit of a cushion.

Dusk is closing in as I sit with legs crossed and weigh my prospects.

Really? What prospects? One thing I need to do is to take out my contact lens and save it somewhere safe. It was more valuable to me than diamonds at this point.

Without it, I'm nearly blind, anything more than a foot away nearly indistinguishable. Even walking would be dangerous because I'd never see the hazards - boards with nails, jellyfish, sharp rocks.

I can't let it blow away or swallow it. I should find a tiny bottle or container to put it in. I study the beach for anything that might work. I spy one of those flimsy water bottles! With a cap!

I hunch over in my nest and pop the lens into my cupped hand. I lick it clean for good luck and drop it into the bottle, screwing the cap tight. I tuck the bottle inside my bathing suit top. That's pretty safe! Nobody's been there for years!

"Come here, Raisin, time for bed," I call. "Here's a treat, come and cuddle with me."  She turns in two full circles and stretches out next to me, her hairy warmth a huge comfort. I listen for the start of her gentle snores and close my eyes. Please god, don't let me die, I mutter. So true.

# CHAPTER 28

Even from 100 yards away, Jim looked stricken.

He was standing on the Whaler's broad bow seat, arms akimbo, knees bent for balance. His ball cap was gone and wisps of gray plastered his head.

His eyes were huge as he looked at the kiddie pool that moments before had been an unsinkable Boston Whaler.

Three bags of fishing floats we'd found on beaches floated away on the current, along with treasured driftwood I insisted we bring home. Nothing that floated was left. And he was drifting further away.

I cupped my hands to yell. "Throw the anchor! You have to throw the anchor!" The brutal current in this part of the Abacos would sweep him out to sea in minutes. Jim dropped to the floor of the Whaler and found the small aluminum Danforth. He pitched it towards the big boat and the Whaler snugged up and stayed put.

I was frozen. My eyes were the only part moving, my mouth agape, my hands clutching my head like the face in the painting. The Scream.

Jim's panic raced across the water like a living thing. I couldn't see the details, and I couldn't begin to wrap my brain around his paralyzing fear of what had happened.

He crouched lower in the Whaler, which was completely awash. The fuel tank was tethered only by its line, and was floating like a party balloon off to one side. Only the top few inches of the motor showed.

I raced into the salon and grabbed the microphone to call a Mayday. West End was so close, surely someone would hear. I tried the emergency channel, the fishermen's channel, the cruisers' channel.

"Mayday, mayday. Calling any boat. Sailing vessel Wham B'Ama in distress between Grand and West End…. Mayday, mayday!" But nothing. Not a whisper.

Jim showed signs of life. He shoveled water out of the boat with cupped hands then realized he did have help. He lifted the middle seat and started sweeping the water out, maybe a gallon at a time. He looked like a crazed cricket player. Swipe, splash, swipe, splash, swipe, splash.

I shouted encouragement, and eyeballed my own situation. We were in a tough current. The big boat leaned heavily on the anchor.

If I tried to get closer by kedging - tossing the small anchor as far forward as I could, then pulling the boat towards it - I would more likely drift further away in the current, or lose control and end up stuck in the sand.

I tidied up the mainsail, and piled it neatly back on the boom so I could raise it again when I needed to. I fastened the halyard and made sure it wasn't caught anywhere on the mast, and when I looked again, Jim had the Whaler half emptied.

He was losing steam though. The seat wasn't picking up as much water, and he had to scoop it higher to get it out of the boat.

His dark, freckled back glistened with sweat and salt water as he leaned into the task. Swipe, splash… swipe, splash… swipe, splash. He was exhausted and moved like a robot. Swipe, splash…

I could only watch. Raisin lay on the deck next to me, nuzzling her last but one tennis ball, mouthing it like a newborn puppy, then letting it roll a few inches and snatching it back.

The Whaler was too far away to be of interest. She could fly 20 feet if she thought it meant a trip to shore, but 100 yards? Not worth a glance.

***

Jim finally stopped bailing with six inches of sloshing water left, and shifted his attention to the motor.

He gently pulled the floating gas tank back into the boat. The emergency oar had floated off with nearly everything else.

If he had to, Jim might try using the seat as a paddle to reach the big boat. But that would be brutally tough, fighting the current, no hope of going straight. So the motor was his only hope. A scant few tools had survived in the anchor locker.

He took off the motor's housing and started outboard CPR, removing the spark plug and blowing it dry, dumping the carburetor and air-drying the plug and hose that carried the gas to the motor. From my seat of enforced idleness, it looked complicated and hopeless.

It wasn't just that we were 100 yards apart.

Without the Whaler, the big boat would never make it off the banks and into the ocean. A narrow, badly marked dogleg channel makes reaching the open ocean under sail impossible even with a maneuverable boat.

Page 58

Wham B'Ama is big, heavy, and slow to turn. She'd never make it sailing against the current, even if the route were straight. Which it's not.

And without the Whaler, even if we made it into the Atlantic, we'd be pulled north by the Gulf Stream and reach Georgia or the Carolinas.

And without the Whaler, we'd never make it into an inlet. And without the Whaler, we wouldn't make it to a bank to get some money to pay for a towboat.

I could only shake my head. Nightmare. Worst nightmare.

Jim had been laboring for over an hour to dry the motor, an impossible task with salt water.

He rinsed the parts with gas hand-pumped from the can. He finger-wiped gas into the hole for the spark plug, and sucked and blew on the end of the wire, and splashed gas into the carburetor.

In another hour, he'd put the parts back in and fastened the housing. He'd had nothing to drink and had been sweating with the heat and his labors and his fear for hours. If a heart attack was his destiny, now would be the time, I thought.

He plugged in the fuel hose and grabbed the rope handle to pull-start the engine.

Three pulls was the general rule, but the rule was out the window now. Three pulls. Squeeze the bubble thing. Three pulls. Squeeze again. Nothing. Three pulls… 30 pulls. Nothing. He was ready to drop.

Plug, out. Housing, off. Spark plug, out. Wait…. Dab with precious gas. Wait…. Spark plug, in. Housing, on. Plug, in. Rope, pull. Pull. Pull. Sputter! Miracle! Wait! Pull. Pull!

Sputtering sputtering sputtering. Silence. Shit! Pull! It's running! Ohmygod!

Jim hung onto the tiller with one hand and edged forward to pick up the tiny anchor, then spun to head for the boat.

He looked like death, pale with sweat streaming down his face. He reached the big boat and grabbed the side with the line in his hand, and stepped onto the ladder with rubbery legs.

He fell, exhausted and shaking, into the cockpit. I handed him a cup of water and the bottle of Bacardi Black. The water disappeared, and he upended the rum bottle with shaking hands.

"Never. Never again," he mumbled. "I'll never get on another boat." But he did. We did.

# STORM

# CHAPTER 29

# August 2, night

Like Andrew and Bertha and Jean and Frances and Wilma and Katrina and Michael and Dorian and Ida and I don't remember how many others, this unnamed monster was twice as bad on the back side.

I slammed my head so hard on the bulkhead that I must have lost consciousness because I was thrown around the cabin like a rag doll, waking on the floor crammed next to Jim.

Not only did the roiling waves hurl the boat up and down like a hobby horse, we were pitched from side to side. Making it worse, the anchor line would relax and then snap tight. We were in a 40-foot blender with no off button.

On a downward surge I managed to crawl upright and grab the dinette seat, then rocket onto the seat as the boat tipped the other way.

I couldn't tell if the salt on my face was tears or sea spray. I feared my life was ending, and knew I couldn't survive much longer like this. I just couldn't hang on. The world was pitch black, in constant terrifying motion, and every inch of my being screamed in pain.

It had been 19 hours. I had nothing left to save myself. I gripped the table and lay my head on my arms. "I can't. I just can't."

# ISLAND

## CHAPTER 30

## August 8

But I must have.

But what? Did the boat sink? Was I washed overboard? Did I fall? I awaken to blue sky and questions, and to Raisin doing her salute to the sun, a double stretching thing she did every day.

I'm convinced she must have practiced yoga in a past life. Woo, thirsty. And not a drop to drink, as they say. That's got to be the first thing.

"We've seen worse, right, Raisin?" Probably not, I think, but I'll keep her spirits up. "This is a new adventure, eh? Let's go pee."

She romps along the sand and picks her spot. I step out of my salt-stiff shorts and walk knee-deep into the water. No muss, no fuss, just a splash or two and I'm done.

I go back to my little shelter and try to finger-comb my tangled hair. Hopeless. Yank some more. Grab a bunch and try for a braid. Maybe I'll find some string.

Now to find my contact lens. Careful! I reach into my suit and peel the bottle away from my sandy skin. I spot the lens. Smooth, tiny, rounded.

I turn against the wind, shielding the bottle as I tap its opening against my palm. Thank god for an opposable thumb, I think as I secure the lens and slip it into my mouth. Salty and just a bit gritty. My tongue anchors the lens while I swallow the grit and generate clean spit, then pray for a few moments of still air.

I lick my finger clean, bend over to shield my face and pop it in. Forty years of practice, but nearly always with a mirror. No such luck now. Is it in? Did it blow off? I open my eyes and blink. A bit scratchy, but I can stand it. My tiny world springs into focus.

Now to look around, find something to eat. And water. Another coconut. I'm already exhausted. In a little while, I think. I curl up again on my mat to rest and dream of better days.

An hour later I stand up feeling nearly normal, except for the tortuous mosquito bites. The blasting hurricane wind apparently didn't phase them, and they were starving! As was I! It was my second full night of sleeping in the nest of seaweed and pine needles I had cobbled together on a flat and protected sliver of the rocks.

Yesterday I had been in such pain from the punishment of surviving, I could barely move. So I mostly rested and found some freshwater puddles, thanks to Raisin's talents. I had to beat her to them before she lapped them up! I rinsed some of the dozens of plastic containers stranded on the beach and scooped as much fresh water as I could.

Near my hidey hole, I position my treasure among some fallen branches and cover them to keep the water relatively clean. I've managed nearly three gallons in assorted plastic cheese containers, Tupperware, Gatorade bottles and one actual gallon water bottle. With a cap!

I set aside the broken jugs and plastic bottles I'd picked up, and the biggest prize of all — a leaking one-gallon water jug. That was a real treasure, and I made a special hole in the sand to position it so the leak stopped.

"We have to pray for matches, Raisin," I tell my sandy companion. 'Get those paws together and give a shout to your doggy god! Ahwoooo! Ahwooooo!"

After the doggy prayer and a Parmesan cheese container of water, I call Raisin to me, tried to ignore that high-pitched mosquito whine, and slip into darkness.

# ISLAND

# CHAPTER 31

# August 9, morning

So today, I need to figure things out. "Boy, I'd love a coffee, even it was black," I tell Raisin. "Even without sugar… well, maybe." On the boat, if cigarettes and dog food were Numbers 1 and 2 to demand restocking, half and half for my coffee was a close number 3.

Of course, half and half was a distant dream, even if I were standing in the middle of a supermarket in an actual town, like Marsh Harbour.

The best I could hope for was reconstituted milk, which had a weird taste I had actually grown to relish. It tasted slightly better than the dry milk powder that was a staple everywhere, even in the tiniest closet-size out-island shop.

But even the milk powder was more palatable than the canned evaporated milk. Either way, I had grown so used to the chlorinated water in the boat's tanks — a safety measure I probably overdid — that the concoction I ended up with resembled coffee only in its color.

More than coffee, my stomach is trying hard to reach my backbone… two days on the island and at least a full day in the storm too terrified to eat. Another small container of rainwater helps and I wonder if sea grape leaves are edible. The grapes make jam! I might be in luck!

I stand and stretch, surprised that everything moves as it should with only a few twinges. I shrug off my jacket and look for a limb to hang it on. No such luck, so I give the precious water containers an extra cover and head to the beach for a rinse.

Raisin bounds after me, excited for the movement. She stops in my path with a hopeful look and a little bark.

"Oh Raisin, I wish I had something for you… I'm hungry, too, kiddo. We'll get lucky today… crabs? We know there's lots of those, right? Maybe we'll find a fish that's not too gross… can you find a coco? coco?"

At the magic word, Raisin's ears rise up and her eyes scan the beach.

Coconuts are one of her favorite things in the world, maybe even more than her tennis ball. She can husk a green coconut in under five minutes, ripping the tough green husk to pieces before attacking the even tougher white string protecting the treasure inside.

All the while, she whimpers and yelps, ravaging the husk to reach the brown, hairy coconut inside.

Once she had it, she would roll it. And roll it. And roll it some more, for what seemed like hours, and until her nose was bare and bleeding.

When we stole it away, we'd shake it to check for milk and try to open a hole. The natives made it look so easy. It's not.

The nut inevitably splits and the milk spills, but our prize was the juicy meat inside… especially the young nuts that weren't yet hard. Their meat was like pudding, delicious.

"Oh, stop thinking about food!" I yell out loud. "Wash your face and just shut up! Think about Tom Hanks… he had it worse!"

I enter the water, cool but not cold, and my scrapes are healed enough to not hurt. I strip off my shorts and bathing suit and give them a saltwater bath, too, watching three days of sand sink to the bottom where it belonged.

I scrub my arms and legs and then float to let my hair rinse as well. Against all odds, feeling clean was joyous and I snug my bathing suit back on and walk back to the beach. I had stashed my contact lens in one of the containers I'd found and I need it to be able to see more than my hand in front of my face.

I try to keep the lens out of the grit as I rinse it off, then suck on it as a last hope for cleanliness, then duck under my coat to put it in my eye. Losing it would be a disaster. I blink and feel just a bit of scratching. II hope  for the best.

"Let's go, Raisin," I yell. She was 50 yards down the beach, digging her way to China. "Come on, we have to find the boat. We have to find Jim! Let's go!"

She bounds towards me, ears flapping, tail streaming behind, leaping like a gazelle to reach my side. 'Thank god for that dog,' I think, not for the first time. I rub her face and smell her panting breath. "You're such a good girl!"

We head to the area of beach where I should see the boat. I reckon the tide is still high from the storm, but lower than the day before.

Maybe I can spot the mast if she's gone aground somewhere else on the island. The standing, leafless trees would make it hard to pick out the mast, but nature abhorred a straight line, they said…

"Who are They?" I ask Raisin for the thousandth time. "It's always They. They this. They that…  and a lot of times They have it wrong! The earth isn't flat even though for millennia, They said it was! Don't get me started!" She snorts in agreement and lurches off again into the shallows.

Page 64

We reach the end of the dry sand, and enter the cluster of mangroves that surround the southern reaches of the island. Inside the mangroves - if I can get there - I'd never spot a mast. I have to try to go around.

I never had, even though we'd been there for months. I ventured into the ankle-deep water and was happy to see tiny minnows. If all else fails, I might net some and hold off starving. I could use the hood of my jacket, I think.

As the sun climbed higher, the water climbed as well and it was harder going. I can't see the end of the island. Raisin is leaping and swimming, chasing tiny fish when she spots them.

'I wish I had that energy,' I think. 'This is brutal.' Another 200 yards and my legs are cramping from high-stepping like a marching  band's drum major. I was exhausted.

I try floating to rest but my legs won't work so I edge onto a mangrove knee and sit. Raisin finally looks tired as well and leans against me in water up to her belly.

" Ok, kiddo, we're done here. This is too far. We're gonna head back and make another plan. You good for it? Yeh? Good girl!"That faithful tail wags and those trusting eyes light up.

We were off.

The return trip seemed easier, and I figured the tide had peaked and was going out. The tides in the Bahamas are odd because the island groups surround a saucer-like shallows in the middle of the big bowl of ocean. When the tide comes in, it's from all directions, like pushing the floating saucer down so the water overflows the edges. Confusing, because nearly all of the island chain is on the same schedule. And the "inlets" can be deadly.

# MAIDEN VOYAGE

## CHAPTER 32

We were anchored in Tilloo Bay, one of my very favorite spots. We'd been there for weeks, and I'd spent hundreds of hours snorkeling and watching the conchs and other creatures etch winding paths in the pure white sand six feet below me. Except for the sea life, the pristine bay was flawless, protected, silent, and too shallow and boring for the party cruisers.

For Jim, he was as happy as he would ever be, smoking his packs of cigarettes in the cockpit, buried in his war novels, the male equivalent of Harlequin books. For me, like watching ants or a beehive or a hummingbird, I was transfixed by the life underwater.

But on this day, it was calm after a front came through and kicked up the ocean. We knew "junk beach" would be full of treasures - glass, sea beans, bottles, and lots of floats from all over the world. Glass balls, lead balls, lots of styrofoam, plastic of all kinds, from a ping pong size to a basketball... we couldn't resist gathering them up.

The good thing about junk beach was that it belonged to some friends who lived in a tiny cottage on the bay side.

The bad thing about junk beach was the 30-foot dune between the bay and the ocean.

Coming back with bags and bags of found treasure was brutal. So on this day, we decided to take the Whaler out of the cut and pull it up on the beach to avoid the climb and collect what we knew would be a trove of great flotsam.

We nosed into the cut, and saw the rolling whitecaps filling the space. Jim gunned the motor a bit and I grabbed the side of the boat, ready for a rough ride.

Raisin was in the bow, her front legs on the seat that held the anchor, nose up to sniff the wind and ears like flags behind her. It was rough, as rough as we had seen except for that ride in to shore at the start of Hurricane Michael.

But we plowed through, climbing and dropping, up and over the rollers that were getting bigger as we entered the ocean, rather than smaller.

When we cleared the inlet and saw the beach, we just stared. Although the wind had dropped, massive breaking waves were hitting the beach. There was no way to land the Whaler, or to get back out if we did manage to get ashore. We'd have to turn around, a nasty prospect that has sunk many a boat caught crosswise in the trough.

From the other side of the island, we had been lulled by the protection of that 30-foot dune that blocked the wind still gusting about 25 miles an hour.

Spray from the whitecaps was blinding and Jim angled the Whaler across the rollers to lessen the motion, but the waves seemed as close as train trestles, or those expansion strips on a bridge. Too close.  It was a terrible spot… we had to get out far enough so that when we turned around, we would be able to reach the inlet and not be driven onto the beach and sure disaster.

Disaster awaited in the inlet, too, but with slightly better odds. I knew better than to offer advice, but I had none to give.

Raisin was enjoying the ride. Jim was white as the proverbial sheet, gripping the throttle like the lifeline it was. We were finally out of the breaking surf and into the rollers.

"Hang on! THIS IS IT!"he yelled. We slid down, down into the trough, and I looked up, up, ohmygod up at the wave towering over us. Jim was turning the Whaler into it.

For what felt like minutes, the Whaler was near vertical, everything loose slid to the back and piled near Jim's legs. My legs clamped on the seat in front of Jim and I doubled over to grasp the side of the boat with both hands. Raisin was still on all fours in the front. We climbed, climbed and … if we didn't reach the crest before it broke, we were done. A curl of white signaled the break, we reached the top of the wave and…

We dropped like a meteor into the next trough, 12 feet but it felt like the Grand Canyon. The gas can flew out of the boat, tethered by the fuel line.

I went airborne, three feet above the seat, and landed on my knee on a round lead float. Precious bags of treasures flew out and returned to the ocean. Rusty lifted up like a helicopter from the bow and slammed back down onto the deck on all fours.

Somehow, Jim's grip on the throttle kept him in the boat and he managed to retrieve the gas can all the while angling us back toward the inlet. But now the waves were behind us, and we were traveling with them. The worst was past.

# MIKE

# CHAPTER 33

# August 9, morning

MIke surreptitiously eyed his watch. Late again, he thought. The hurricanes this summer were killing him.

He'd been flying American's Orlando/ Cape Town, South Africa, route for seven years and late arrivals had never been this bad.

He didn't even know the name of this storm. Orion? Nancy? Last week it had been rocketing through the Bahamas, expected to peter out. Now it's causing havoc in northern Florida and Georgia.

As one of a handful of flight attendants with more than 30 years in, he had his pick of routes. In spring, he jockeyed for the long ones that he worked back to back a few weeks at a time so he could spend the summer sailing his precious Prout catamaran.

The 24-hour Cape Town trip, or his other favorite, Rio de Janeiro, racked up enough flight time for him that he could spend at least three months in the Bahamas. Even long weekends were doable if he could hop the right flights. But the best was when he could patch together a couple of unscheduled months and have enough time to enjoy the distant islands.

"This is your captain speaking," finally blasted out of the speakers. "Sorry for the delay, but we should be landing shortly. Please place your tray tables…" Mike tuned the voice out and unclipped his harness to start patrolling for unfinished drinks, trash, the odd sound sleeper.

He glanced at his watch again. 'I just might make that connector to Great Harbour,' he thought. This was his third week of nearly constant long-haul flights and he was past ready for some clear water, blue sky and Kalik beer.

In the last 12 weeks, he'd been in the air for ten. But the packed schedule, and the weeks  he'd already stockpiled  gave him more than three months of freedom before he had to go back to the friendly skies.

This summer had been a brutal one for his schedule and his normal May departure had slipped to August. This was his last scheduled flight and it's late.

If he misses the flight to Grand Harbour, he'll lose four days until the next one. It'll be tight.

He buckled in for landing and minutes later he was smiling at the restless passengers. "Thank you so much for flying with us…. See you next trip…. Can I help with that bag?… Thank you for choosing…."

# ISLAND

## CHAPTER 34

## August 9, morning

I feel almost human. Maybe I'm getting used to that stinky soft spot, I think. The last of the clouds had swept away the miasma of humidity and if the circumstances had been any different, I would call it a gorgeous day!

"Not a joke, Raisin! It's gorgeous, right?" She bolts along the now familiar strand and angles into the calm water. I follow and strip everything off, even my crusty bathing suit, and join her. I stay close to the beach, floating in gin-clear waist-high water and rubbing sand out of my hair.

"Come on, Raisin," I yell. "We can walk around the island. Let's find Jim, eh? Where's Jim?" With a yelp she races back to me and wiggles impatiently while I struggle into my wet but not sandy bathing suit.

"You just don't know who's out there!" I caution. "We don't want to scare them off! Let's go, kiddo… maybe we'll find a Waffle House. They're always the first to open after hurricanes. Right?"

We set off toward the less hospitable, mangrove-filled end of the island. I think if the boat had dragged in the storm, it could have wedged itself into those shallows and survived.

Jim could be stuck with a broken leg or worse, just out of sight and reach.

Surely there's some sign somewhere of the boat, I thought. It's 40 feet long and the mast is nearly 50 feet high! How can it be missing?

The long debris-ridden beach gives way to the mangrove forest and mucky shallows, making travel difficult. Distances are deceptive in this clear air, and I figure the beach stretches nearly two miles.

Now in the trees,  I can only lumber through waist deep water 15 feet from the clusters of roots, slow going.

Or I can struggle through shallower water impeded by dozens of mangroves and a gummy bottom sucking at my sand shoes. I try to split the difference, keeping my eye peeled for Raisin's wagging tail.

I plod forward, batting mosquitoes and looking at the sand bottom for a likely conch or shellfish I might eat. As I wonder again about Raisin,  I hear her yelps in the distance.

Another coconut? Then a loud bark. I still can't see her around the sweep of the island, so I move closer to the mangroves and try to move faster.

Raisin's barks continue and as I clear a bend, I see what she did ~ what looks like a beached whale just clearing the surface of the water.

Wham B'Ama on her side, mostly underwater, about 50 yards out. Only her broad belly shows inches above the quiet water, the pilot house, the deck, everything else submerged.

Her broken mast bobs close by, held in place by the sturdy wire rigging that once secured it.

A slick of leaking oil and diesel stretches from the boat to the mangrove-riddled shore, offering a rainbow of color on top of the clear water. As I follow the slick with my eyes, I can see bits and pieces from the boat trapped in the roots and branches.

It's too far to make anything out.

Holy shit. Raisin has managed to find a muddy patch away from the water and sits quietly. I'm in knee-deep water, hanging on to a mangrove branch, paralyzed. I can do nothing.

I have on my sand shoes but can't risk a swim through diesel.

For one thing, Raisin would follow me, a disaster, and she would never stay behind. The diesel would burn like fire, and without soap, would never wash off.

Jim had either made it to the island or was drowned inside the boat. Or washed away, I think, like me. I try to remember just where we had been anchored, but so much was a blur.

I thought we had been at the other side of the anchorage, closer to the beach where I fetched up… no, this is at least a mile away and she's closer to shore.

I think back to when the wind switched. I can't remember everything, but I can imagine a line snapping and poor Wham B'Ama impaling herself on the coral.

But now I had to figure a way to get to her. Food! There are cans still inside, and bags of rice and pasta. Drinks! Wine! Praise whatever's holy!

I mentally  check through what might survive being submerged. Jim either made it or he didn't. If he's on the island, he'll appear.

Otherwise, he's gone. I need to live. I need some food!

# MAIDEN VOYAGE
# CHAPTER 35

Anyone who has spent even a day on a sailboat knows that Topic Number One is inevitably favorite things to eat. Not sex. Not movies or books. Food. Favorite foods, favorite cookies, favorite drinks, what you'll eat first when you get to shore.

Eighteen hours or 18 days or 18 weeks, it's the same. Just a matter of intensity. It's a mental trick because all you'll get is what you have with you - no Starbucks on the corner, and no Publix or Golden Arches. So your dream is for what's not there. What you just can't have.

"Oh, I'd love a steak," someone will say, glaring at their peanut butter sandwich. "I'd love some real half-and-half for my coffee," would be next. "Ice cream. I don't care the flavor. A gallon. Just for me."

The likelihood of finding any of those items in the Bahamas was right up there with winning the lottery. Two days in a row.

But it was always fun to dream. After months in the more remote islands, where a shop the size of a Ford van sold eggs by the singles and boasted of having an onion for sale but carried five-pound bags of rice for $1 American, my dream was for what I began to call "knife meat."

We had lucked out in our last visit to what passed for civilization and, I had snagged a cabbage and a couple dozen packets of outdated sandwich meat, each one normally intended to make one sandwich.

With imagination, pepper sauce, a lot of rice and just two wafer-thin slices of mystery meat, I could turn out a palatable dinner. I could make one packet of meat last at least three days!

If we reached what the Bahamians called a supermarket, I might manage a pricey and long-frozen chunk of something that had been red at some point, but it, too, was hoarded and carefully sliced to give the barest hint of flavor to whatever was cooking.

"Fish?" You ask. "Fish?!?" I drop into my best growl. "We don't have no effing fish!"

After thousands of dollars in lures, line, spinners, weights, rods, hooks, nets…. Squat. Zip. Zero.

If a fish actually tickled the hook, a barracuda was right behind and we'd pull in a ragged head. We lucked into a big fish once, and he ran off with the hook, line, sinker and rod! I fondly remembered the John McDonald book, "The Girl, the Gold Watch, and Everything." The barracudas got everything.

Eventually, the fishing gear morphed into my personal entertainment system. I'd hook a chunk of bread and dangle it over the side of the Whaler then don my mask and stick my head underwater so I could watch an array of colorful fish nibble away.

Even the remoras that had adopted the big boat would wander over, showing me their odd sucker-like heads, then sniff the hook and turn in evident disgust.

So on arrival back in civilization, where recognizable pieces of meat were available and affordable, they landed on the dinner plates in one piece. They required cutting, they were so big!

And "knife meat" was celebrated for ever after.

# ISLAND

# CHAPTER 36

# August 9, afternoon

I realize I should call out for Jim, but my voice is stuck. I croak, breathless, my throat seized up as reality settles in.

"JIM! JIM!! ARE YOU HERE?" Raisin chimes in, much louder, her bark traveling at least a mile. But only silence and the lapping waves respond.

I stand for nearly an hour, watching the diesel slick, judging the distance, trying for a plan. Any plan. The shock of finding the boat has fried my brain and I can't grasp a thought before it whips away, replaced by another.

I'm too hungry for this, I think. First, I have to find another coconut and get some energy. Wham B'Ama isn't going anywhere.

I unclasp my fingers from the branch and yell at Raisin. "Come on, girl, let's go. We're going home now." She bounds over the roots and into the chest-deep water to lead the way.

As I reverse course and slog back through the deeper water, I wonder at Jim's fate. I wonder if whatever power there was had finally heard my nightly beseeching.

# MAIDEN VOYAGE
## CHAPTER 40

Our relationship, and I use the term loosely, was not the greatest. It's a boring, ordinary story, except for the boat. We met, hit it off, had separate boats that we each sold to buy Wham B'Ama together.

I was earning the best money of my life working for a crazy national supermarket tabloid, traveling often for work while Jim hung out, cooked dinner and acted as house-husband. His Army pension kept him in cigarettes and beer.

Things were fine while we worked on the boat and I put in the time to get fully vested in my company retirement plan. Jim was kind, funny, social, affectionate, chatty, all that stuff. Until…. Guess what?

Here's the age-old story. I quit my job and my income stopped. Suddenly he was the breadwinner, took control, turned surly and became a person I no longer knew. Sadly, a person whose name by then was alongside mine on the title of a boat I had sunk all my money into… a boat I was determined to cruise in, and so was he.

So we formed a truce of sorts, finished the preparations and headed out. We each had our duties, our books, our separate thoughts, determined to make the least bad out of a miserable situation.

As the months rolled by, the small aggravations became monumental. Living on a 40-foot sailboat offers about the same room as an average parking space. It doesn't get much closer.

So at night, after yet another frustrating day, on our opposite sides of the V-berth, I would lie awake and listen to Jim's ragged breathing.

Maybe I should ask the almighty to forgive me now, I think, for making that plea night after night.

As I'm moving through the knee-deep water, I can feel the sun cooking my shoulders despite the dark tan I already had.

Yep, I confess, I'll say it. It became a mantra. I'd listen to his light snores and utter a silent prayer: "Please, God, let this be his last breath." It wouldn't be, and I'd whisper it again and again until I finally drifted off. Needless to say, his breathing continued. So now am I supposed to feel guilty if that wish came true? Will I celebrate if I find him alive and well?

"I can't think about it," I murmur aloud. "I'll be like Scarlett. I'll worry about it tomorrow."

# ISLAND

## CHAPTER 39

## August 9, late afternoon

As I clear the mangroves and trudge along the beach I spot something red tangled in the seaweed at the tide line. When I reach it, four of those ubiquitous red plastic beer cups are peeking out of the damp mess, stacked and ready for a party.

I carefully separate them and rush to the water to make sure they don't leak. They don't! Each one of them fills up!

"Raisin, lookie here, kiddo, a miracle! Cups! We'll make water!"

I remember a trick I'd seen where a leaf releases its moisture into a cup or a plastic baggy; not a lot, but we had four cups! Without holes! And maybe we'd find more! Suddenly, my exhaustion and hunger disappear as I feel a sliver of hope. We might make it.

After we reach the beach, Raisin finds another coconut - lunch and dinner. By now I know the trick of getting the nut open. A check of our lucky moon rocks yields enough water to survive.

No such luck with the cups though. I struggle to fasten just one over some sea grape leaves. I finally manage to braid enough grass together to make a string to hold one cup in place, but a puff of wind blows it off, and it doesn't look like it would work anyway. The other three cups are wrapped up in my jacket. I won't get to them today.

I need a plan to reach the boat. As the sun edges closer to the horizon, I abandon the water project and gather up some dry leaves and brush to reinforce my bed. The island is smothered in drying leaves.

I'm still hungry, parched and thoroughly exhausted. My beach strolls and swimming over the last few months have done nothing to ready me for this.

I was never a jock, always the last one picked for any game. The first for spelling though, or book reports.

"Fat lot of good spelling does me now, eh Raisin?" I grumble. "I should have learned to climb that goddam rope and run a mile." Her golden eyes give me a loving gaze.

The sun's eyebrow slips its last millimeter… no green flash, again. "Raisin, come on, we've got a bed tonight." She ambles over, equally tired after a tough day. I slip my lens out and carefully store it again before kneeling into my leafy nest and rolling onto my side. I reach over Raisin's back, feeling her tail wag against my legs at my hug.

I feel her warm breath and the enormity of the disaster suddenly strikes me. In an instant, my optimism flees and I know in my soul I will die on this island with this dog.

My throat closes and I sob the tears of the completely bereft. My arms and legs feel an electric shock of terror and I double over to trap my heart inside my chest.

I cry and cry for all the joy I'll never see and all the mistakes I'll never get to make. Exhausted, drained I fall into the sleep of the damned.

# ISLAND

## CHAPTER 40

## August 10, morning

When I struggle awake, the hollowness of devastation is not as fierce. A silent, solid determination to survive fills the cracks. I have to reach the boat. I have to find some food. That's all there is to it. My English "stiff upper lip… get on with it!" upbringing is kicking in.

I was 4 when my parents and I left Coventry -  birthplace of Lady Godiva and home to Jaguar Motors - for Canada, then Connecticut, then Arizona.

After surviving nightly bombings in the Blitz - industrial hub Coventry had it so much worse than London - followed by years of near-starvation under rationing, my parents sought greener pastures. But that didn't mean they gave up any of their "Englishness."

Dinner conversations inevitably turned to disparaging America and Americans, despite it being their chosen home. Parents were too soft, women bossed their husbands and spoiled their kids (heaven forbid), the education system was a disaster, the population at large was generally ignorant, people ate things like mayonnaise and peanut butter, they bought their clothes instead of making them.

My mother made everything we wore, ironed everything, cooked everything. Badly. I celebrated the tastes I discovered in my high school cafeteria - Cole slaw, mystery meat over rice, American goulash. Delicious! Flavor! Not boiled!

My father was typically stoic and disapproving. If I had five As and a B on a report card, his first comment would be: "Why do you have this B?"

I don't recall a single word of praise until far into my adulthood.

Nevertheless, this determination to survive and their unwavering demand for perfection served me well in times of stress. Like now. "Stress" being the understatement of the year.

So I brush off the leaves, seriously consider tearing out my tangled hair by the roots, and walk into the still water for my morning ablutions.

Raisin is a half-mile down the beach, in a nose-to-nose confrontation with a crab. My throat is still raw from sobbing and my eyes feel puffy from the tears but I can't waste time. I have to save myself.

August 10, late morning


The slog to the boat is quicker this time and it's still morning when I reach the spot where I had been the day before. I'm armed with my jacket, some big sea grape leaves the size of dinner plates, and one of the precious red cups.

My plan is to first explore the detritus from the boat caught up in the mangroves. It ranged over quite a distance, some deep into the roots, but worth a look. I need to keep an eye on the bottom, as well, for things washed overboard that wouldn't float. Cans, tools, even books for paper I could dry out and use to start a fire.

As I venture forward, the first thing I spot is a small fender from the Whaler, a tough airfilled cylinder that keeps one boat from crashing against another.

The lines had caught high up in a mangrove and it was hanging happily from a limb about 50 feet away. It was a clue for the direction other flotsam had taken. A harbinger! A chuckle escapes as I realize my vocabulary has survived. So far.

It also told me the water level had been a good 10 feet higher than it was now. No wonder Wham B'Ama was all the way over, I realize. She rode the storm surge in and just fell over when the water receded.

As I near the fender, I spot another not quite as high and 30 feet further into the mangroves. Halleluyah! That's two huge problems solved!

I thread my way through the curved roots and tattered branches to reach the further fender first. It was easier to reach and not as wrapped up.

Not as punished by the wind and waves, I realize. Its line was a single piece through its center, about six feet long. I just have to undo the knot at one end to get it free and I can tie up Raisin while I get to the boat!

I clutch my prize like my firstborn, and make my way to the second one. I tie the first to a root so it won't float away and scramble up to loosen the knots from an upper branch. Twigs and leaves and tight twists - a result of spinning in the wind - make the going hard.

I hang on with one arm and reach up with the other to try one-handed to release the line, rotating the fender to loosen the rope and picking out bits of wood and debris as it untwisted.

Finally, it pops loose and I fall backwards, barely missing the jumble of roots below.

As I reach to grab the fender, my eye catches a flash of color on the bottom. Red. Where? The disturbance from my feet clouds the water and I lose sight of my prey. I stand like a statue to let the sand and muck settle and there it is, caught under a low root. Campbell's!

I step forward and lean down, my arm out and my face in the water. Stuck! I lodge the fender between my legs and move as close as I'm able to the can, but roots are everywhere, small, large, in and out like a giant's knitting.

I kneel this time and reach out both hands but I'm still too high. Dunk this time, hold breath, pitch forward, grab can.

Pull! Ooof! Damn! Again! Yes! One more! Holy smokes! Beef with barley! Not my favorite, but it will be wet! If I can open it, I realize…. Later. Later.

Now I have to reach the boat. "Raisin!" Her bark comes from the dry spot she found the day before. Perfect! Here I come, and you're not gonna like it, I whisper to myself.

The dog is a mind reader. If she suspects she will be tied up, she's off like a flash, out of reach until I succumb. Not this time.

I carry both fenders by their lines, dragging them floating behind me. Why on earth did I bring the cup? Small stuff, I think. And the leaves? To wipe my face, some protection from the diesel.

The soup is jammed inside my bathing suit for safekeeping. The cup and leaves I stash inside my jacket and cinch the waist tighter.

I reach Raisin's perch and plop cross-legged next to her to work on extracting the line from the first fender. Less of a mess. I shed my coat for the moment and feel the light breeze on my damp skin.

Raisin puts her head down and relaxes as I work. Finally, the knots clear, I pull out the rope and I'm ready. I nuzzle Raisin's ears and cheeks and slip my fingers under her snug collar, quickly securing the end of the line and tying a nice, firm knot.

"Good girl! What a good girl!" I praise her, standing up and tying the rope end to a convenient branch. "You have to stay here. I'll be back. Sit! Stay!"

She hasn't been tied up in a year, but her struggle is halfhearted. She's hungry too, probably more than me. I hope my visit to the boat will cure that for both of us.

"Get on with it!" I can hear my father's voice, gravelly from decades of pipes and cigarettes.

Now I have one fender with no line that I need to secure somehow, and one with a line that I'll use to help me reach the boat.

My plan is to swim around the diesel slick as best I can, and try to clear it in front of me when I can't.

Page 81

I'm hoping my jacket will protect my shoulders and I'll keep my hands high enough so the water won't travel up the sleeves.

Hanging onto the fender will help with that, as well as the swim. My neck would be the problem, and I can't see a way around the likely burn.

"Stiff upper lip!" I say it to myself this time.

I wedge the fender between two branches and put my jacket back on. The cup goes into a pocket and the leaves inside my suit. I put the soup in there as well, rather than risk it falling out or leaving it behind. I snug up the Velcro sleeves and collar and walk into the water.

Twenty feet past the mangroves the bottom drops out and my feet lose the bottom. My jacket balloons as I settle into position with the fender in front and my legs kicking me into deeper water.

Wham B'Ama must be in a hole to be lying the way she is, with her keel broken or gone.

The going is slow and I'm wary of any current that could pull me the wrong way. Too many sailors had disappeared like that.

I wish for a long line but that's a pipe dream. "Just watch out! Lions, and tigers and barracudas! Oh my!" I whisper, still well clear of the slick.

I reach the curve of the hull with just a faint stinging on my hands from diesel splashes.

My neck is spared, thanks to the fender's help supporting my head.

The water is lower today. A full foot of the hull is exposed and the occasional wave reveals the edge of the pilot house and cabin.

The receding tide took most of the diesel with it. Now to see what was what.

The broken main mast angled into the depths, the naked boom end bobbing near the surface. I try to look into the water but I'm too close. I need some height.

I splash the water to disperse the diesel, then pull the fender down between my legs and straddle it. Balance!

I rock against the hull, my legs gripping the fender trying to pop to the surface. If I lean against the hull, I can just manage to stay on and see where I am. Cabin windows maybe three feet! I can stand!

I grab harder onto the line of the fender and loose it from my legs. It launches itself to the surface as I extend my legs and touch a frame. I hug the cabin side, half floating, and ease my way right, toward the cockpit, toward the main hatch and the door. Toward god knows what, I think.

# MAIDEN VOYAGE

## CHAPTER 40

I must admit, that maiden voyage wasn't all death and despair. There were some high points.

The early summer had been filled with storms and threats of storms. Some interrupted the annual Abaco regatta, a 10-day round of seven races and raucous parties, each at a different island. The normal program had been pared down to three because of a hurricane threat and the last race was on the barely populated island of Guana.

Guana had a postage stamp-sized harbor we had visited weeks earlier, and spent an hour picking a spot to anchor because two boats were already there.

Jim and I weren't racing, but we were partying… free food, free drinks, music. When we nosed into the tiny anchorage we saw at least 50 anchored boats and more coming behind us. A long jumper could hop all over the anchorage and never get wet.

Everyone had faith in their anchor, and their neighbor's anchor. When the tide changed, the boats would all reverse direction. If one boat's anchor line was 90 feet and his neighbor's was 40 there would be a big Ooops moment, inevitably at 2 a.m. when they crashed together.

We held our breath and settled in, then dinghied ashore for the last party of the regatta.

Liquor suppliers - primarily rum - donated the oil that lubricated the parties. This party had clean-up duty, and had four parties' allotment of liquor thanks to the cancellations.

Dozens of half-gallon bottles covered tables that separated the band from the sailors. Tiny plastic cups were stacked next to five-gallon pails of ice. A handful of cases of Coke and tonic languished under the tables.

Spiced rum, dark rum, white rum, Jamaican rum, Bahamian rum, aged rum. Take your pick. There was so much rum there wasn't even a line to get a refill. Nobody missed the soft drinks when they ran out, or the ice.

It was the night I discovered Anejo.

I'm not a dancer. I was never a jock, always awkward, can't hold a beat. Uncoordinated. In concerts, when everyone is clapping away, I'll look around and realize I'm clapping to my own beat. I stare at my hands like foreign objects, pause, and have to start again.

But this night, four Anejos in, I was a dancer. At seven Anejos, when I had five more lined up on the table because it was rumored the liquor was running out, Jim announced he was leaving.

"I'm not! I'm not leaving!" Somewhere my brain noted a bit of a slur.

Jim pushed the handheld radio at me.

"Call me when you're ready. I'll pick you up."

I stayed near the back, trying to count my stack of empty cups. But I was having trouble. The music kept interrupting.

Then the band started playing "Hot, Hot, Hot," a perennial favorite, the Bahamian equivalent of Mustang Sally that gets everyone on the dance floor.

The chair I'd been sitting on looked pretty solid and I wanted a better view. Just one small step more and I was on the table, dancing my heart out, less inhibited than I'd ever been with clothes on.

***

Earlier that day, I'd had an up close and personal look at that final race.

I had bumped into Sarah, another woman who loved sailing, on the Marsh Harbour fuel dock. She had been with her on-and-off boyfriend on a 45-foot racer but on the day of the final race, she had broken up with Frank yet again. She was waiting for a taxi to the airport. We promised to stay in touch and she reached into her purse for a card when she discovered her passport was missing.

"Oh no!" She dumped her bag on a nearby bench. No luck. "I left it on the boat!" She was stricken.

She was flying home, desperate to not spend another minute with Frank. He had dinghied her to shore, bid her good riddance, then left to join the four dozen boats jockeying for position near the start line for the race. By now it was well under way.

I had a handheld radio with me, and a crew member answered when Sarah called Frank.

"She can get it when the race is over," the crew relayed Frank's answer. "We're not stopping."

It was about 11 in the morning. Her flight was at 3. The race wouldn't end before 4. The boats were competing in Abaco Sound because the ocean was too rough on this wet and windy day.

Jim was ensconced on Wham B'Ama with his coffee and smokes. I was feeling pretty cocky on my own with the Whaler.

"Come on!" I said. "Let's chase him down!" We piled into the Whaler, Sarah in the bow to pick out the boat, me finally able to pull-start the motor. I eased away from the dock and headed for the distant cluster of boats racing around the buoys.

The bay was rougher than I realized, three-foot rollers with the wind blowing off the tops. We hobby-horsed toward the mass of white sails, cold salt water soaking us every few minutes with a rogue wave.

The racing boats were fast - moving away from us, of course - but we were faster. Despite the rough ride, I was standing, my knees acting like pistons to keep my balance, hand gripping the tiller extension to control the motor. It was a thrilling ride!

Sarah called on the radio to see where Frank was in the fleet, but no one answered. Frank was as competitive as they come and would sacrifice anything to win. No doubt every crew member was cranking or getting ready to tack or judging the distance to the next buoy.

We caught up to one of the last boats in the race and asked where Frank's boat was. "Way ahead, way ahead!" the helmsman pointed and gestured.

I pulled away from the slower boat and plowed back into the swells, up and over, up and over, dodging around and through the racing boats, hearing their curses for getting in the way and giving a friendly wave back.

Sarah finally spotted Frank's boat 200 yards ahead of us. Frank hadn't acknowledged Sarah's radio call that we were coming to meet him and get the passport. Did he not hear it or was he just being the ass he was? We didn't know.

We finally drew close. He was racing hard at about seven knots, rails down, the huge jib full and driving them forward, going for the boat's greatest speed. The Whaler was plowing along at about 10 knots, being swamped every minute or two. Sarah and I looked like drowned rats. Her nice traveling outfit - even topped by her foul weather jacket - was a distant memory.

We closed on the high side of the boat. We risked being run over if we approached on the low side. Sarah yelled, I yelled and Frank finally glanced away from the wheel and saw us. "Fuck this," he yelled back.

Sarah begged, "I'll never ask you for anything else! This is it. You're rid of me.

"But I have to have that passport!"

Frank reluctantly sent one of his crew inside to find it. As we waited, I moved away from Frank's boat and dodged two others closing on us. The crew guy emerged and waved us over, passport in hand encased in plastic sandwich bags. He looked at us, then at the passport and disappeared again. When he returned, the passport was in a big plastic jar with a red lid.

I uttered a small prayer of thanks. If he missed the whaler with his throw, we'd have a chance of finding it.

Frank was still at the wheel, cursing under his breath at the interruption to his concentration. Sarah and the crew member were sharing the blame. I edged as close as I dared, hoped this guy had a good arm, and gave him a signal to throw.

Halleluyah, the cannister landed in the middle of the Whaler. We wouldn't have to fish for it.  Sarah threw herself on it like a football player in the end zone. We waved and shouted a thank you to Frank and the crew.

I slowed the motor and picked my way through the rest of the fleet to head back to the dock. Sarah zipped the passport into a pocket, ran her hand through her dripping hair and gave me a big thumbs up.

# ISLAND

# CHAPTER 41

# August 10, afternoon

Wham B'Ama is settled on her side, so I have to think of the space inside turned 90 degrees. What was the cabin floor is now vertical - a wall - and completely underwater.

I was heading toward the doorway which is now horizontal, and hopefully open. The cabin windows are the new ceiling.

As I edge along, the small salon windows I've been walking on give way to the huge plywood-covered pilot house windows. I can see them clearly two feet below, and as I move closer to the back of the boat I see the open hatch and the bi-fold entry door flapping lazily in the moving water. I can't make out the piles in the corners of the cockpit - tools?

Whatever it was, it was all too heavy to float. I see the mizzen mast still in place, the boom lashed into the massive crutch at the stern. I can make out its length below the surface of the water.

Getting inside will be easier than I thought. The boat is wide open. But my contact lens! I know I can't open my eyes with it in. Here I am, in boat soup! How will I ever get it out?!

I slow my thinking and look at options.

Swim back? Then what? There's no place to leave it on shore. Go into the boat blind and feel my way? How would I find the way out?? No way. Try to get steady enough to take it out and put it away here? Possible. Pocket. Inside pocket.

Paper from the soup can.

I pull the soup can out of my bathing suit and examine the clinging label. I peel it away, finding a section with no glue. It seems sturdy enough. I have to risk it, so I balance myself, bend over against the slight breeze, and pop the lens into my hand. I quickly clasp my fingers and shield my hand and the paper with my body.

I carefully wrap the lens, fold over fold over fold that I pray won't unwind in my pocket. No!

Not my pocket! The bra inside my bathing suit!

It's perfect, as long as I'm not moving too much… secure enough so the paper won't unwind and float away! Okay then!

I reach down and unzip my jacket, then feel inside my suit for the bra. I feel the opening between the elastic bottom of the bra and the stretchy fabric of the suit and wedge my origami packet in between, near the top, close to the strap. Perfect! Or as perfect as I can hope for.

I can no longer make out anything in the distance, but I can see well enough to find some more cans inside the boat. If I can hold my breath, never my strong suit.

I edge further back and deeper toward the cockpit, grabbing the cabin top winch - which helps tighten the lines for the sails - and tying up the fender. The jib winch against my foot tells me I'm a step away from the cockpit seat, now vertical.

My next perch will be the horizontal inside frame of the door, but I can't figure the depth. I grab the fender rope and ease myself over the coaming into the abyss.

I float near the open doorway and push the bi-fold door more open with my feet. I can stand easily with my head and shoulders above the water. The fender line is my security blanket, but I can grab the cabin side as well.

The hatch over the doorway is open so my body fits three feet inside the boat, floating vertically. I stand on the side of the first dinette seat and easily reach the surface.

What luck! I can't see inside the boat without ducking my head and opening my eyes, which I hate, but I can feel. The table has fallen, one side down and one side trapping the cushion I was exploring with one foot. Still closed. What's in there? I can't remember.

Damn, this brain that knew where every screw and screwdriver was! What the hell was in that compartment? Later.

I wonder again where Jim might be. I wonder if the open door meant he had left the cabin and gone into the cockpit for something and was swept overboard.

It was a relief I hadn't found his body. Even though my feelings for him were far from warm, I didn't want to find him dead.

I wedge my elbows and raise myself up so I have a better angle to see into the water. Sure enough, there was the table. The varnished tops of the steps into the main salon are gone, off on their own voyage into the unknown. Everyday tools still there, of course, but toppled out onto the half-wall of the galley - now the floor. Not rusty yet.

Page 88

My moving around disturbs the diesel slick, and I feel burning on my arms. I swish it away and take another look. I need cans! I need a can opener! I can't see into the galley from where I am. I can see into the main salon, though, and except for the swirling mayhem, it's empty.

No Jim. Gone. He surely thought he'd make it to shore. Or he fell. Either way, he must be gone from this earth. I utter a small prayer to whatever god he believed in. Probably none, I think, as depressed a guy as he was.

I hope his next life is happier.

I resume my appraisal.

Lots of things floated trapped against the windows, now the submerged ceiling of the boat. Food wouldn't be floating, but I think I can see that crazy four-foot plastic horn.

I look deeper. A bag of split peas leaked its contents over a cupboard door, now the floor. It would be sodden and congealed, but edible. Treasure!

Nearby, a shiny pile — contents of the silverware drawer. A knife! I look again at the detritus near the ceiling. Plastic bags! Yes! What else? I look to the settee, still in place but with everything that had been on it scattered. My precious watercolor of a wind-tossed sailboat is still attached to the bulkhead, its vibrant colors now a blur.

The tangle of sails, rigging, jackets, have been stirred like a stew and settled where they landed.

It's too soon to think about sorting anything. I just need a few necessities to survive and I'll take it from there. The soup, some ropes, a tarp if I'm lucky, the peas! The knife! Those grocery bags! Enough. My eyes are already bigger than my belly.

I edge as far into the open hatch as I can and steel myself for the dive. The surface with its diesel is the scariest. The jacket will help me sink.

I cover my face with one hand, take a huge gulp of air, and reach the decorative galley upright to pull myself under the water. I squint to spot another handhold and haul myself far enough to reach the bag of peas.

I grab the bag, losing some precious grains, and pop to the surface, one hand hanging on to the small bag and the other shielding my eyes.

Now? I cling to the door frame with my feet and hold up the bag to find its leak. Small.

Enough to let water in, but only a few grains out. No worries.

I unzip my jacket and jam the bag inside my bathing suit next to the soup can and zip back up.

I feel for the wrapped lens and it's still safely tucked in. Now for the knife!

I repeat the process, easier this time, and manage to grab one hefty kitchen knife and three spoons. When I reach the surface, I realize the knife is a problem. I can't hold it and continue my gathering. Sorry, B'Ama, I mutter. I jam the point of the knife into the door frame.

Safe. Until go time.

Now for the bags. I slip under the surface again and edge my way along the windows until I feel the flimsy plastic. Got 'em! Now for a quick peek!

I'm floating horizontally against the cabin windows, a handful of grocery bags jammed into a jacket pocket. I squint to see greasy tools rolling against the settee back, the seat gently rising and lowering with the boat's movement.

A flash of bright green beneath a sail. Seven-Up! I'll never make it! I can't kill myself for a Seven-Up!

Above the back of the settee, wedged into the bookshelf, my man overboard bag. That heavy sucker didn't travel far at all, just the floor changed. It rolled with the punch!

The cockpit cover and poles are still wedged near the floor, too many fixed obstacles for it all to move far. I might be able to pull it out, I think, and make a shelter. Tomorrow.

I push backwards to the cockpit, out of breath. Is there any air space in there? I stand on the coaming and rest for a bit, deciding what to do next.

# MAIDEN VOYAGE

## CHAPTER 42

There's always a next! Sometimes a good next, sometimes not so much. The day Jim did his salsa dance on the sunken Whaler just happened to be Thanksgiving.

A celebration wasn't at the top of the list when he got back to the big boat.

By then, the tide was outbound and we couldn't risk being swept out to sea. It was too late to call for a tow into the marina, and we couldn't pay for it anyway.

Jim grabbed a blanket from below and huddled into a fetal position on the cockpit seat. He stayed where he could smoke. He was on his last pack, which he had nursed for three days. I wasn't surprised he was going through withdrawal from his normal two packs a day. At Bahama prices, it was a $500 a month habit.

I retired below to take stock as well and started digging out the Thanksgiving surprise. Precious.

Eureka! I found everything for the feast… Ritz crackers and a few slices of sandwich meat for the main course. And for dessert, the surprise… the "sleeve" of Oreo cookies. Both are too rare on the little islands to squander an entire box, so the shopkeepers parcel them out by the sleeve, wax paper or cellophane sealed, and not yet softened by the relentless humidity.

We dined in silence, emotionally and physically exhausted from the weeks of terrible weather reports and the strain of towing the big boat.

Most safe anchorages were a day's sail apart in good weather, but this was the summer that hurricane names ran out and we had been under near constant watches and warnings for months.

Even now, we were constantly advised to stay put. Days and weeks went by as we crawled our way west. The noise from the two constantly running gas motors was mind-numbing and the fumes inevitably blew into the stern.

We were both cooked brown from the sun and incoherent from exhaustion on that Thanksgiving Day off West End.

# ISLAND

# CHAPTER 43

# August 10, afternoon

I decide to risk a breath up near the ceiling - the windows - in case there was an air pocket. I edge again into the main salon and grab the side of the hatch to eyeball anything I could identify.

A big porcelain-clad mixing bowl was rolling in the galley, spilled from a cupboard along with a frying pan and a sludge of paper plates. A sodden box of kitchen matches dumped its contents nearby. I think I see another can.

I turn my face upward and feel air on my face. I take a couple of deep breaths - deep for me after years of asthma - clamp my eyes shut and pull myself into the depths. I have less than a minute.

I reach bottom and squint my eyes to see the bowl and frying pan. The pan first, tucked under my arm, then I grab the bowl. Where's the can? Nope! The matches then, before I explode! I burst out of the hatch and know I'm done for the day. Another try and I'll screw something up, and I still have to swim back.

I catch my breath perched in the doorway and unload my treasures into two of the plastic bags - bowl, matches, frying pan, peas, soup, spoons. The knife is a problem. Too long, too sharp, but the thing I need the most.

I zip my jacket back up, then tie the bags as tightly as I can and shove them inside. The mixing bowl and frying pan barely fit. I unwind the fender and position it near my neck, my left arm clamped to keep it in place.

I pull the knife out of the cabin frame and carefully nest it against the fender, one hand on the hilt and the other hand flat against the blade.

I kick off the boat and slowly paddle my way toward shore. Ten feet from the mangroves, I drop my feet to feel the mucky bottom and stand up.

Nothing lost! I shift the stash inside my jacket and snug up the waist tie as I stand up. I release my death grip on the fender and pass the knife handle to my other hand holding the line for the fender. Contact lens? Yes, I can feel the paper with my lens still safe near my shoulder. I utter a small prayer.

Raisin's distant yips direct me - the trees are a blur without my contact - and I march toward her little rise. I collapse onto a mangrove root as she wiggles and licks an ecstatic welcome.

But joy is short lived as I judge we only have two hours before the sun disappears. First, I need to be able to see.

I slip off my jacket and my treasures fall out. I reach down inside my suit, then back up towards the strap and seize my precious origami. The outer layers are mush but as they disintegrate, the solid inner layers appear. I undo the last two wraps of paper and my lens is there, safe and sound. I give it a good swish in my mouth and lick the sand off. I turn away from the tiny breeze and shield my hand. Wow! Trees!

I untie Raisin's rope and bundle up my finds inside the jacket. I tie the arms like a pack, and hook it over a shoulder. "Let's go! No time to waste!" I shout as Raisin bounds into the water..

# August 10, late afternoon

I'm filled with anticipation on the trip back, dreaming of tasty peas with a whiff of beef barley flavor. I have a bowl, something to put in it, and a knife to pierce the can.

"All's right with the world, eh?" Raisin is leaping through the shallows, chasing her new favorite toy: a small school of baby sharks, their floppy fins bobbing in and out of the water's surface.

We reach our spot. Our last night here, I think. We need to move closer to the boat, less time to walk and more time to retrieve whatever I can. Maybe I can rig a winch to pull B'ama closer to shore… later.

We reach the nest and I dump all my treasures onto a sea grape leaf carpet to assess: I put half the bag of soggy split peas in the bowl and walk over to the shore for water to cover them. They are already soft from their few days in the sea, but I think the setting sun might actually cook them a little.

I eyeball the soup can, sadly not one with a pull top. I look at the blade on the kitchen knife. Plenty sharp and pointy, but tough enough to put a hole in the can? I wonder.

I'll cross my fingers. I lay out the handful of sodden matches. Those are truly precious, I think. I thump my chest, grunting. "Me make fire, Raisin! Me cave girl! Uh!"

I grab the can and look for a safe place to secure the matches. I slip them under a heavy stick, hoping they'll dry. Next I find a solid spot to wedge the can.

I aim the knife and drive it into the lid. A tiny divot appears but no hole. Again. Another divot.

I grab a nice rock, baseball size, and position the knife tip in the first divot. Bam with the rock! And the can weeps a drop or two of beef juice.

I can't resist, and quickly lick it off, then reposition the can and whack another hole, bigger this time. Another tiny flavor explosion!

By now Raisin's powerful nose alerts her from a half-mile down the beach and she races to me in hopes of a decent meal.

While the peas "cook" in their seawater, I decide to risk picking some greens to try. I should have paid more attention when my pal Lupe walked me around that tiny island in the Berries, I think. She knew them all, and there wasn't much that didn't go into her salad or soup pot.

I snag some new growth that has emerged since the storm and give it a nibble. More arugula than butter lettuce, I think, but it has vitamins. I pull a few more stems, and something else with a broad leaf that smells like basil.

By now the sun is lowering and I can't wait any more. I shred the greens into the pot and dump most of the saltwater before pouring in a couple tablespoons of the soup stock. "Give it a nice little stir, eh, Raisin? Just like Jamie Oliver tells us? Would he like this dish, just a few things from the cupboard?"

Raisin is salivating at the smell. Me, too. I grab a spoon from the pile of treasures and give it that magical stir, then scoop up a tiny amount of peas, a flake of greens and a hint of gravy. Heaven! Better than the best five-star restaurant I'd ever been to, after three days of nothing during the storm and three days of coconut.

The peas are actually soft - not soupy soft or mushy peas soft, but certainly edible soft. The leafy stuff adds a tang and the hint of beef is a blessing.

I know to not gobble the whole thing... that would spell alimentary disaster. And I need to share. So when about a third of the bowl is left, I let Raisin inhale the rest. For dessert I send Raisin off to find a juicy coconut while I rinse off the dog licks in the waves and bring a little water back.

I finally sit, relishing my not-famished belly and plan for tomorrow. I'll get close to the mangroves and make another camp, I think. We'll eat more peas in the morning and have some energy. I pour half of the remaining peas into the bowl to keep soaking, then organize our meager belongings for a speedy departure. I wrap the precious soup can into a sleeve of my jacket to keep the critters out and make a nice stack of everything else before turning toward my bed. Raisin assumes her position, spoons into my chest, and we're asleep before we see the first bolts of lightning in the northeast.

**Page 94**

# FREEPORT

# CHAPTER 44

My first real cruising experience was back in the day when lonely sailors advertised for a partner in sailing magazines like Cruising World. Over many months I had sent off a dozen or so responses, and finally got an answer that sounded interesting.

Most letters, in indecipherable scrawls, came from older, broke, divorced, miserable guys. They had bad spelling and worse sentence structure. Ok, I'm a grammatical snob. It's a deal breaker.

Then a legible, coherent letter arrived from a guy named Arlen. We chatted on the phone and he had a voice like Southern honey. The photo that arrived with another letter a week later showed a golden, lanky guy with sandy hair and a drop-dead smile.

I threw caution to the wind and flew to the Bahamas for two blissful weeks on his trimaran.

But I'm getting ahead of myself.

Arlen met me at the airport with flowers and a taxi waiting.

He was taller than I'd pictured and had shoulders way too wide for the tropical shirt he was wearing. He grabbed my bag and ushered me out of the small Freeport airport. The humidity hit me like a sauna. I'd been in Phoenix for two years and always felt like a raisin. In the humidity I felt like the grape.

We drove the 10 minutes to Arlen's trimaran, tied with a dozen other assorted boats on a sea wall in a part of Freeport called Lucaya. It had once had a famous resort, now closed despite a decade of promises to reopen.

In the meantime, Lucaya had two less fancy hotels, a dive shop that offered certification and lots of trips, and a small restaurant upstairs called The Tide's Inn.

Arlen's boat was spartan, the kindest word I could use. He had built it himself from plywood and aesthetics - or comfort - weren't high on his list.

But it was functional, clean, tidy, and he said it was seaworthy enough for the world cruise he wanted me to share.

He showed me into the guest bunk area, showed me the toilet and how to use it and cautioned me not to let the water run in the sink while I washed my face or brushed my teeth.

"The tank only holds 40 gallons, which sounds like a lot, but it's not," he warned.

We sat in the cockpit while he grilled some chicken and heated up some rice for our first dinner.

I was nervous, tongue-tied, and Arlen filled the space with tales of how he'd built the boat in his North Carolina backyard, how cruising was his dream, how hard it was to find a partner.

With dinner over but the night still young, we walked up to the Tide's Inn for a glass of wine and to meet the "family," the very mixed bag of neighbors and friends.

Any new arrival was in for close examination - to be questioned, prodded, poked, looked at, studied and finally approved or not. Passed off as boring or snooty. Or embraced as an entertaining addition.

"Did I play backgammon? Bridge? Dive? Was I a nurse?" Apparently nurses were in high demand. Whatever I'd said turned out to be right because I was accepted with flying colors, offered use of a bicycle while I was there, invited for a variety of outings.

I had no chance of remembering the names of my dozen new friends, just one woman about my age, and the rest men 10 to 40 years my senior.

Most looked pressed for cash. A couple appeared to belong under a bridge. And one or two seemed pretty flush, drinking top shelf liquor instead of $3 wine.

They took turns transfixing me with tales of island life, especially the social highlights. The two hotels in Lucaya each hosted a weekly cocktail party for guests.

The parties featured free rum drinks, a dance contest to Bahamian music, and a few bad hors d'oeuvres. The key word being free.

The boaters would amble in with the hotel guests and lap up the freebies. The hotels tolerated this because the boaters added an ambiance to the party, like monkeys in the zoo.

Not only that, lots of the guests were single women, at least for the week, and most of the boaters were single guys. A good time was had by all.

# FREEPORT

## CHAPTER 45

With stars in my eyes, I quit my very good job, rented out my house and returned to Freeport a month later to begin my new life sailing the world. The "cruise" lasted three days and never left the dock.

Arlen was supposed to meet me at the Freeport airport. In Fort Lauderdale, at his request, I had picked up two massive sails, gallons of paint and epoxy, tools, lots of food. He didn't show. It took two cabs to carry me and the supplies to the marina. Which at 1 a.m. was locked. It took an hour of yelling to wake someone up to wake up Arlen. Not an auspicious start.

The next day he told me he'd decided not to stock cheese for sandwiches, just peanut butter. We'd had this discussion.

"I hate peanut butter," I had told him on my first visit. "I've always hated peanut butter."

But on my return, his answer was, "You'll just have to learn to like it. Cheese costs too much."

The day after that he got into a snit because I hadn't sold my house, just rented it. "I'm not ready to burn that bridge," I told him.

"We need the money!"

On my first visit I had been befriended by the tiny group that lived on boats tied along the sea wall in Lucaya.

It was quite the circus. The longtime "leader" was Shep Meyer, a middle-aged sailor who owned a half dozen boats under constant repair. He was tall, 6'2" at least, filled out a speedo like a Greek god, and had legs like polished oaks.

Every morning he would poke a newly picked red hibiscus into his ratty straw cowboy hat and patrol the beach for the ideal woman. Rich, slim, beautiful, young, single and sexy. Did I mention rich?

He never found a girl to match the long-gone Lorelei who had briefly filled the bill. Shep's memory of her perfection doomed any human woman who might show interest. That didn't slow his daily search.

Next was Wolfgang, a tiny German guy who had emigrated to Canada and was a builder. This was his first Bahamian winter, a big improvement over Toronto snow. Wolf loved working on his boat, and helping others do the same.

One day someone passing through needed help with a masttop fitting, and sent a friend off to fine a bosun's chair, a contraption that lifts someone up using the line that would normally raise the mainsail.

Wolf overheard the discussion and asked what the job was. Two lines had become crossed and just had to be straightened.

In a flash, Wolf jumped onto the boat and shimmied up the mast like a monkey. He yelled from the top, his legs clamped and one arm clutching the mast while he waved and yelled for a consultation about the lines. In seconds, he had fixed the problem and slid back down the mast. The fellow going for the bosun's chair still wasn't back.

Cheap John lived on the sailboat behind Arlen. It hadn't moved in years, and the deck was piled high with pure, unadulterated trash - empty bottles, plastic grocery bags, leaking gas cans, rusted tools, discarded boxes - that John regarded as treasure.

He was another Canadian, small, thin, always in shredded denim shorts and a long sleeved white shirt so threadbare it was transparent.

As he rode his heavy single-speed bike the white shirt would blow out behind him like a sail. He was compulsively tight and never spent a penny. He lounged for hours every day drinking water in the tiny water's edge restaurant.

The oddest of them all was Fritz. He was by far the oldest, past 70. He had been a Nazi in the war, designing and repairing guns and other weapons. He came from a family of watchmakers, his profession before and after his service. His big sailboat had been anchored 100 feet off the seawall for decades. It didn't run, had no sails, looked bad even from that distance.

Fritz would row into shore in a barely floating dinghy and buy a coffee that he would nurse for half a day. Sometimes he would comb his long white hair and most days he shaved. I doubt he ever washed his shirt or pants. Personal grooming was not a priority.

Fritz talked with a heavy German accent and a surprisingly big smile. His bright blue eyes sparkled like Christmas lights as he explained in minute detail how a watch worked, or almost anything mechanical. His meager income came from repairing clocks or small appliances that people brought to him.

Fritz was equally entrancing about food, German of course. To hear him tell it, he was an artist with strudels and other pastries. He never talked much about the war, but unselfconsciously admitted he'd been an officer under Hitler and performed his job well. His amazing posture spoke to years as a soldier.

On the third day after my arrival Arlen told me he was going to take another woman sailing instead of me - she had arrived with her boyfriend in the weeks I was settling my affairs at home. Her boyfriend had left her, but the boat was his so her days were numbered. And she liked peanut butter.

This crazy group had witnessed the drama between Arlen and me like a daytime serial. So when I walked off Arlen's boat with my suitcase behind me and my dog in my arms, intending to fly home, every one rallied to my defense.

They cajoled, persuaded, offered solutions. They all wanted me to stay. The best offer came from Shep. He said I could live on one of his boats, Khayama, a 1920s gaff-rigged sailboat, free in exchange for my promise of two hours work a day. Another offered me a spare bike.

Such a deal! I was in my mid-30s. I had been working nonstop since age 16 in a a series of newspaper 24-7 jobs. I had some cash, now an old bike with a milk crate in front to carry my dog, a place to lay my head and a new life. Hell, yes!

# CHAPTER 46

B'Ama wasn't my first encounter with a Newporter 40.

Hunky Shep Meyer lived on one, and let me stay on her when he was out of town. I just fell in love with that boat, and wrote love letters about it to him.

"I'm curled up on your cozy couch, entranced by the gleaming wood of your beautiful boat," I told him. "She is perfect!"

Shep was preparing her to sell, which meant hauling the boat out to paint the bottom and a trip to the infamous Cracker Boy do-it-yourself boatyard in Riviera Beach. Shep enlisted Fritz and me for the passage, which I didn't know would be the first of my "Trips from Hell." The first of many.

When Fritz and I "crewed" for Shep, the departure was delayed… but I learned in later years that nearly all departures are delayed for one reason or another, for anywhere from an hour to a month.

Nevertheless, we learned quickly that we weren't sailing a boat.

"Zis is an oil painting, not a boat," Fritz grumbled. "Zis is a showboat! Zis man iss crazy!"

We finally left on a Saturday, Shep with a hellacious cold and fuzzy-headed after handfuls of cold pills, Fritz at the wheel and barely able to see with seven-year-old glasses, and me assigned to go below and organize a walking space through the mountains of junk destined for sale in Fort Lauderdale. Shep had collected parts, screws, propellers, motors and miscellaneous detritus now piled all through the boat.

The first adventure was the visit to the fuel dock, where a disabled boat blocked where Shep wanted to pull in. Of course.

It was Fritz' and my job to hold us off the pilings and protect the gleaming varnish while Shep pumped the fuel. He didn't want to use fenders… they might mar the paint! No worries that we might lose a finger. The first bit of excitement came when Fritz failed to follow Shep's instruction to the letter… the yelling and waving and glowering and fuming that followed proved to be Shep's pattern for the next two weeks.

He didn't want to use the motor - in case it broke, no doubt - so we hoisted the sails in very light winds and crawled along at less than two knots toward West End. It took more than 12 hours to reach our destination and anchor off the channel. We ate a cold dinner of bologna sandwiches and I discovered the only drinking water was in a pickle barrel. Never a fan.

Then another boat anchored close by and Shep spent the next four hours watching them through binoculars in fear they might be pirates and attack us in the wee hours. To Shep, everyone was suspicious.

In the meantime, I went to bed amid the joys of a hermetically sealed (and very hot) boat. "No bugs!" Shep yelled. "Keep those hatches closed! No, don't open the windows!"

Fritz opted for the coolness of the cockpit. About 1 a.m. we discovered he suffered from night terrors, loud and disturbing, in Russian and German, as he fought off imagined attackers.

We all got up before sunrise and I discovered Shep also outlawed use of the stove. No propane on the boat. "It might explode!" He pronounced. "No generator! Too heavy! It uses gasoline!"

So the menu for the trip - breakfast, lunch and dinner - was cheap white bread dry bologna sandwiches and pickle-flavored cold coffee. Yum!

We neared the Florida coast after what felt like years of sailing, but we were north of the Palm Beach inlet. Not good. This happened because the Gulf Stream flows north at about two to three knots, so as we slowly sailed due west, the current carried us north. When Shep saw our position, he fired up the motor and headed south. At three knots. We motored all night, gaining nothing, all eyes straining into the darkness to pick out landmarks and navigation lights.

When dawn came, Fritz stepped up with a reality check as Shep was holding steady two miles off the beach. We may as we have been anchored for the progress we were making. We watched the same roof for six straight hours.

Fritz's guttural German accent and wild pointing at the shore finally won the day and Shep reluctantly increased the engine's speed and edged closer to shore.

We reached an anchorage and Shep hitched a ride on someone's dinghy to the boatyard. We had to be cautious because Shep was telling Immigration that only two people were on the boat. We were smuggling Fritz in with a long-expired passport and no other identity papers. He was under orders to leave the boat as soon as we reached shore and not return until dark.

The next day, I drove Fritz to the German consulate in Miami. He was so nervous, and so overwrought when he was explaining his predicament, I thought he was going to have a stroke. But he left with a shiny new passport, and the comfort of knowing he was legal for the first time in years.

"Naaah, not to worry," he said, with that sly twinkle. "Not to worry. It vas all an act. I did not vant all the red tape, so I pretended I vas a pitiful old man." Which he was.

"Tonight! Ve vill celebrate!" That night, he treated Shep and me to dinner. He even wore a clean shirt.

So years later, when I saw another Newporter for sale, she had to be mine. But I was glad she hadn't been Shep's.

# ISLAND

## CHAPTER 47

## August 11, early morning

Rain! Freezing dollops of rain pelting my face wake me up and I shove Raisin out of the way so I can stand up.

I rip off my bathing suit and let the fresh water sluice away the caked salt and dirt. I spread my suit on a nearby rock in hopes it might rinse clean as well. I pull my jacket and sweatshirt out of my sleeping nest and spread them as well. I make sure the bottle with my contact lens is still secure, then grab the bowl and precious red cups and bury them them upright in the sand to catch what they can.

I'm cursing myself for not planning for this. I realize the sea grape leaves are streaming water and grab a couple of the plastic bags and tie them to catch what they can.

I pause and give my wet body a nice rub all over, relishing the feel of smooth skin instead of grit. Sand was everywhere. And I mean everywhere. As they say, I had sand in places I didn't know I had places. I bent my head over and tried to rub the drops into my hair but it wasn't wet enough yet. I tried to finger out some of the tangles but it would have to wait.

The squall brought with it a 20-degree temperature drop, and the rain was even colder. I shivered and rubbed the goose bumps on my arms. But I relished the feeling and performed a little dance for anyone watching. Raisin!

"Raisin, come here, let's give you a rub!" She lopes over, loving the ocean but hating the rain. I rub her short white fur to dissipate the salt. She cooperates by running off, then rolling on her back in the sand.

I go to see how wet my jacket and sweatshirt were, and whether I can wring them out to get rid of the salt. The sweatshirt is soaked, but rain is streaming off the waterproof raincoat and down the rocks. Yikes! I grab the last plastic bag and direct the flow into it. This is lifesaving. I have extra pounds to live off for a while, but fresh water … now I have to save it.

The cruising magazines always have lengthy detailed articles on how to capture rainwater.

Some people (those without animals, obviously) direct the rain from the decks directly into their water tanks, and filter it as they use it. Even without a dog, I never relished the idea of drinking water from a deck I had been walking on, sitting on, that had been the recipient of diesel exhaust, bird poop, ash from fires, and that had been painted with incredibly toxic substances.

The dog was just the last straw.

Others would rig their awning with a downspout and direct the collected water into jugs or into the tanks.

On a calm sunny day, this seems a great option, so of course that's the one Jim and I chose. I sewed a plumbing fitting into a corner of the waterproof awning, and we secured it nicely with long pvc poles lashed to the rigging.

We congratulated each other on our work and missed trying it out with the first few rains that passed. It was night, we were gone, we were too tired. So when a squall finally approached when we were there, in daylight, and feeling energetic, we happily anticipated topping off the water tank with delicious rain.

What the magazines don't say is that rain inevitably arrives with wind, something we did actually know. So as the rain band approaches, gusts seize the expanse of fabric and lift it, twist it, shake it, and dump whatever water it may have collected onto the poor sucker trying to direct it toward the opening and into the tank.

Once the wind stops and the awning settles down to actually collect some rain, the rain stops as well. There may be enough for a decent glass of rum and rain, my favorite cruising beverage. Which I desperately needed by then.

# FREEPORT

# CHAPTER 48

Lucaya, Grand Bahama, was a place where legends lived, where characters bigger than life strolled the beaches and walked the streets.

The names sometimes told a story of their own. Chopper Smiley, Nick the Greek, George the Pimp and Harry the Horse peopled the daily backgammon boards at the Silver Beach condominium pool bar. They conspired to fleece the tourists who were always eager for a game.

The Silver Beach always drew most of the island's characters.

Chip Shaw was another regular, sitting at his favorite table and holding court with a constant barrage of blasphemous jokes and filthy humor.

Anyone with engine trouble or a broken washing machine knew they could find him there drinking an ever-present Heineken.

Chip was a marvel of a mechanic. His laying on of hands was known to revitalize anything from an Onan generator to a CD player.

He'd be wearing baggy jeans, no matter the weather, and a t-shirt. His wild nut-brown hair blew in the breeze as he surveyed his audience.

"These hands?" he'd ask, lifting them up and out, turning them front and back as though he'd never seen fingers before.

He wiggled those magical fingers. "These hands can fix anything, anything at all!"

Among his current projects was an airplane - small, but an airplane no less - in his living room. It had crashed and he was slowly rebuilding the engine. He was three years in.

Chip Shaw was a conundrum. He was a mechanical genius, but his real job was as captain of a catamaran owned by a millionaire Canadian shoe magnate who only visited a few days a month.

The rest of the time, Chip had the run of his boss' penthouse when wasn't called on to fix everything from planes to aging VWs.

He drank like a fish, but only beer. Had the attentions of many women, but never stuck with just one. Was a skinny, cranky, homely guy, thanks to surviving a plane crash and having his face rebuilt. But with all of that, he won the blue ribbon, the grand prize, the championship trophy in the sack. He made love with an enthusiasm and skill second to none. It was always casual, but holy moley, it was amazing.

# FREEPORT

## CHAPTER 49

Women were scarce in Freeport, at least women who were there for more than a week, and the unattached men were always looking. I was wise enough to know if I hooked up with one, I'd be saying goodbye to all the others, so every man I met went into the friendship column. Almost.

I had learned Fritz's birthday was coming up, so one afternoon as we shared a table at the Tide's Inn, I asked him what sort of cake he'd like me to bake for him.

'No, no, this old man doesn't want a cake," he said.

"Well, I'd like to give you something for your birthday," I said. "I'd like to bake you something. What would you like?"

"He lowered his head and angled his bright blue eyes at me. "I'd like the baker," he said with a sly smile. Of course, he got the cake.

Another day, I attended a wedding between one of the diving instructors and a teacher on the island. All of the island's ex-pats were there. Social events were few and far between, and this one was the highlight of the year.

A small band played and many people were dancing. A 60-plus very tidy gentleman asked me to dance, slow of course. He was a retired Air Force colonel, loved to surf and split his time between Freeport and Fort Lauderdale, depending on where the waves were.

We were on our third dance when he placed my hand on the front of his chest. I stopped in my tracks. My eyes widened to proverbial saucers. What on earth was that? He gave a big grin and opened his jacket. He had a banana in the upper pocket. We both laughed until tears came.

# ISLAND

## CHAPTER 50

## August 11, early morning

So I'm dancing, naked, in the rain, in the sand, wishing I had soap but thrilled that I feel marginally clean for the first time in days. A week, maybe? I look down in the moonlight at my tan lines… white torso, dark chest, darker arms and legs. I look smaller than I remember. No surprise, after days with no food.

"Raisin, are you showing a wasp waist these days? Are you feeling svelte and sexy?" She wags her tail and runs off before I can grab her for another freshwater rinse.

The rain is slowing, following the normal pattern of bluster and noise and retreat. But my big bowl is nearly full, and the plastic bags on the sea grapes are overflowing.

My raincoat is fresher and donated at least a quart of water to the cause. This is at least a week's worth, if I'm careful. Raisin will get her fill from the rocks. It's too late - or too early - to go back to sleep, and I can see a hint of morning clouds in the east.

I dump a bag of water into the bowl, filling it up, than put the bag over it for protection. Then I consolidate what's in the cups. I wring out my sweatshirt - it's soaked, but I think that water would be pretty nasty after what it's been through. Same for the shorts.

So a good rinse will have to do. I give both another squeeze and spread them out on the sea grape branches to dry.

I give the raincoat a good shake and lay it out as well. Last, I squeeze the water out of my bathing suit and debate letting it dry or putting it on.

I look around, seeing Raisin as my only audience, and pull it on anyway. It's good to have someplace to cram things.

As the sky lightens, I think about a nice pea soup breakfast and unearth the leftovers from dinner. The peas are softer after soaking some more, and I smush them with the spoon. I give the can of soup a little shake and upend it to add some beef juice and my gourmet meal is complete. No greens this time, I decide. I'm not sure my stomach was happy with them. But maybe it was the dried peas.

At the smell of the soup, Raisin lifts her head and dashes over in salivating anticipation. I eat my share, then let her have the rest.

I'm determined to find something edible on the boat today, and an opener for the can. The matches are soaked again, or washed away, I think. I'll have to find them and dry them again.

As soon as it's light enough, I'll head for the boat and find a new camp spot closer to the mangroves. I'll have to leave the water… too much to carry now. Yes!

I grab my coat, one fender and the rope for Raisin, and one of the plastic bags. I carry a half cup of the precious rainwater to drink and at the last minute I grab the knife. It was light enough to see the beach and the lowest tide so far.

"Come on, Raisin, let's go see 'Bama!" She bounds ahead, in and out of the rippling sea, off on another adventure.

With shallower water, the trek is even easier and we reach Raisin's muddy rise while the morning is still young. She submits to the rope, and lies quietly as I don the jacket and wade into deeper water. My contact lens is still in its bottle back at the camp, safely tucked inside my shorts.

"What do I want first," I ask myself as I slowly paddle toward the boat. More of it is showing today, thanks to the low tide. I'm thinking I need rope, maybe that roll of vinyl to make a shelter, more matches, a hammer. Food! Anything - cans, plastic containers of whatever, even what's in the fridge. Cheese. Salami! Near the top!

I'd love to find my snorkel and mask, I think. It would make this so much easier. But they were stashed in a cockpit locker, tough to open.

# CHAPTER 51

Months and many hours of work on boats and sailing later, a spectacular 49-foot DuFour sloop anchored in the tiny Lucayan bay, carrying a handsome stranger. Of course.

Within days, I had joined Pete on a couple of day sails, then overnights. Then he invited me on a short cruise to the Berry islands. I was smitten. Of course I said yes. The boat's name, Sans Souci - Without Care - should have been a clue.

Pete was a charmer wherever he went: slim, sandy-haired and bright-eyed. His stories were spellbinding. He'd gesture and grin and act out his adventures in the Pacific or Alaska or Europe.

And unlike most sailors passing through, he had money to spare, nice clothes and a decent haircut. I was too naive to be wary. We'd gone for a few daysails, then overnights, and we were planning a week-long trip to the Berry Islands when he said he had business in Fort Lauderdale and he'd be back in a week for our trip. He left his boat - white as snow, sleek as an arrow with an interior that rivaled any five-star hotel - anchored.

Sure enough, he returned, but this time with another boat. His teenage son was with him on an equally big and spectacular emerald green sloop.

"I'm looking after it for a friend," Pete explained. "It was in the slip next to me, and I couldn't look after it from here, right?"

Pete's crooked smile made everything sound reasonable.

We were sitting in the tiny restaurant overlooking the harbor. Pete's son sat at a distant table. Sixteen and surly, I thought. Too cute for his own good, long, lanky and blonde but with a mouth in a perpetual downturn. Crossed arms over a grubby oversized t-shirt, feet jammed into $2 huaraches.

When Pete invited me to see his new acquisition, I was stunned. Emerald green velvet interior, glistening mahogany, sparkling stainless and brass, silk lampshades.

"The king of Spain had it built for his daughter," said Pete. Clearly, I thought, touching the crystal glasses nestled in the small bar. This boat made even Pete's look like a derelict.

"We leave tomorrow, are you ready?"

"Spare bathing suit, snorkel gear, shorts, shirt, ready!" I countered. Dock pal Cheap John had promised to look after my tiny dog. Of course I had to pay him.

The next morning, Pete picked me up in the dinghy and we set out. His son hauled anchor on the green beauty and followed. The weather was perfect, and Pete spent the time explaining the boat's systems - autopilot, roller furling, the massive winches to raise the main and control the jib.

She was bigger and newer by far than any of the boats I'd been on. The sailors I'd met were nearly all poor or broke or both, working small jobs to earn enough to reach the next port or buy the next beer. Pete was clearly a step above that. A big step!

As we sailed along, Pete talked and talked.

"I sailed all over the Pacific alone for two years… it's big, so much bigger… so many uninhabited islands. Everything is 30 days apart.

"What did I eat? Anything I could find.

"I had the cans stored in the bilge and all the labels washed off, so the contents were a mystery. I could make a kind of flat bread on my one-burner stove," Pete made clapping motions as though flattening a tortilla.

"For breakfast, I'd open two cans. It didn't matter what was inside. Half of each would go between two pieces of bread… I called it a Quixie oven, two square pieces of metal that clamp together with a long handle so you can hold it over the fire.

"Whatever it was, corned beef and pineapple, or canned chicken and apple sauce, sardines and mushroom soup… I ate half for breakfast and the other half for dinner.

"I'd buy a stalk of bananas - maybe 70 or 80 on a stalk - and they would keep me for a couple of weeks. Nothing but bananas. I'll never eat bananas again…"

The stories continued, how he and his girlfriend Elaine had sailed the Sans Souci from France, where the boat was built, through the Mediterranean, their adventures in Portugal, Spain, the Canaries, and finally home to Florida.

"In the Algarve, we'd climb a hill to this tiny monastery with our gallon bottles and fill up with the best wine you've ever tasted. It was almost free. They'd charge more for the bottle than for the wine.

"What happened to Elaine? See these scratches on my back?" He looked like he'd been clawed by a tiger. "We broke up."

Page 111

His crazy stories continued until it was time to anchor. Pete had me furl the huge jib and then the main as he fired up the diesel and we slipped into the tiny anchorage at the southernmost of the Berry islands.

As we rounded a curve of the island, we saw another boat already anchored. As we closed in on it, a couple emerged and waved from the cockpit: a tiny elf of a woman and her tall, darkhaired husband.

Pete waved both arms as we passed, "Greg and Lupe! Old friends!" He explained.

The two men had worked together years before on the underwater oil pipelines in Alaska. The work in freezing pitch dark water with a rubber suit, lead boots and brass helmet, tethered to a surface air supply was brutal and dangerous. It made many men dead, but it also made many men rich. Greg and Pete were two of the lucky ones.

Pete got out after a few years and parlayed his savings to become a general contractor. Greg continued the work until his health told him he couldn't, but by then he'd saved enough so he and Lupe could fulfill their life's dream of comfortably sailing around the world and never working again.

Greg and Lupe had been lounging in the tiny island chain for a month, partaking of the free hamburger dinners thanks to weekly cruise ship visits. Other days Greg would shoot triggerfish for lunch and lobster for dinner while Lupe gathered wild potatoes and greens on the islands. Paradise.

Over the next couple days, I tried to keep up with Lupe's fast pace and faster explanations of what plants were tasty and edible and which to avoid.

She showed me potatoes hidden just below the sandy surface of the islands, tiny berries as sweet as honey, bark that could be boiled for tea.

One night, after a delicious dinner of grilled lobster and salad, Lupe led me into the boat's main cabin where she had a display of tiny skulls and skeletons - birds, small rodents, turtles.

"They're fascinating to me," she said, handing me a beaked head, smaller than a dime. She was right. It was fascinating, so delicate with hair-thin bones, light as a feather. I gently put it back in its place.

"When we're underway, they all go back in the drawer," said Lupe. "But I love my things around me. Just because we're on a boat doesn't mean I have to give them up."

Lupe's voice was so distinctive, surprisingly low and warm for her 4'10" frame. At 5'2", I felt like I towered over her, a rare treat for me.

Every space in the main salon held some memento from their years of travel - carved wooden animals, an ornate cross, feathers of every description, dolls in native garb.

Page 112

Lupe rummaged in another drawer and pulled out a small piece of fabric, round, with an embroidered long-necked bird on it.

"Here, this is for you," she said, stroking dainty stitches. "It's a mola from Panama, made by the Kuna Indians there and in Colombia. We spent many months in Panama when Greg was working. We loved it.

"The natives have created this art for centuries, but it's disappearing as civilization moves in.

"They sew with machines now, but these are hand made. We treasure these."

She pointed to the settee and two pillows faced with large, complex and colorful molas depicting birds and animals of the jungles.

# FREEPORT

# CHAPTER 52

After another day of trailing Lupe and trying to remember her lessons, Pete and I moved on.

Pete's cocky son stole the dinghy on our last night and was hiding on one of the many islands, leaving us with two beautiful boats, no dinghy and just me as the other captain.

Pete took the Spanish boat. "You'll be fine, you know what to do!" He assured me. "I'll be in sight, no worries, just follow!"

It should have been another lesson in Pete's optimism, and how years later I recognized the threat of that smudged black crayon line on the horizon.

Pete's boat was barely in sight when I first noticed the dark pencil line on the horizon.

The line grew thicker and thicker as an hour passed, until it filled the bottom third of the sky. Pete's boat was even further ahead and in the distance, I could see swirling whitecaps driven by a wall of wind. I clipped my safety line to the rail and raced forward to drop the jib and lash it down as the first drops of rain fell.

Within a minute the boat shuddered from a 50-knot blast and black clouds roiled overhead. In an instant, blinding rain and flying spume on top of steep seas were all I could see. The gale overwhelmed the autopilot so I shut it down and clung to the four-foot wheel.

The Spanish boat was nowhere to be seen and I couldn't leave the wheel to reach the radio below and call. I squinted at the compass as rain like icicles pelted my face and ran down the neck of my rain jacket.

I was too terrified to be afraid. I started the engine and steered due north. I winched the mainsail as tight as I could and prayed it wouldn't rip. I knew going north would run me into someplace on Grand Bahama, and safety. I spread my legs and locked my knees against the movement of the boat and my hands kept a death grip on the wheel for what felt like days but was only two hours.

The rain finally slowed and stopped. The Spanish boat was nowhere in sight. I dropped the huge mainsail and motored north. I had lived to tell the tale,

**Page 114**

and I entered the tiny bay to the cheers of friends who thought I was lost forever.

Pete left Freeport the next day, sailing the Spanish boat home first. Rumors soon reached us that when Pete reached his home dock he was arrested for stealing the beautiful sloop. The owner didn't buy Pete's tale of "looking after it," for one minute.

Under his bail terms, Pete couldn't leave Broward County, so his beautiful Sans Souci languished in the harbor for weeks until he found a captain to take her back to Florida.

Many Pete stories surfaced in later months, told by others who knew him better than I. Me? My own Pete stories were more than enough. I didn't regret the lessons. They served me well: Keep a solid grip on the wheel and you'll make it. Be ready for an adventure. Always remember Lupe's island "markets."

# ISLAND

## CHAPTER 53

## August 11, morning

I reach the boat and this time I swim right to the cockpit before climbing aboard. The side of the pilothouse is awash. Still no air pocket, but not as far to reach the bottom. I utter a silent thanks as I tie the fender to the winch, jam the knife into the door frame and decide on my first target.

Easy pickings, I decide, are the things that had been on the dinette seats. The seats are still in place but a tangle of ropes and fuzzy blankets lay against the windows.

I think I can make out at least one sweatshirt, and maybe the yellow of a jacket. Everything moves a little with the motion of the water and I wonder how deep they are. Maybe my toes can give me a hand!

I peer down and stand on the edge of the seat. My head and chest are still out of the water, so I hang onto the hatch and slide down the seat until my feet touch. My chin is about to go under.

I pull back up and take off one shoe and jam it inside my jacket. I repeat the slide and my toes feel the edge of a blanket and the rough texture of coiled rope. I'm still breathing easily so I try to grab something - anything - with my toes. The blanket corner is first, but it slips away from the weight of the rope.

The rope will be more of a challenge. Heavier. My toes are dexterous, but not strong, but I really want that rope. I explore for a piece I can grasp, or that I can shove my foot into and lift.

My head is too low to the water to see, so I'm relying on feel.

My foot finally wiggles into the tangle of line and I wedge one strand between my toes. I lift, jiggle, lift as the blanket does an underwater ballet. They come up together and I back into the doorway with my prize still in my grasp.

I raise my foot and I grab the rope and blanket with my free hand. I feel like I've won the lottery! Yes! I give myself a little applause. I know the rope — braided and about 100 feet long. It's retired from sail duty, but still has lots of life and was the perfect size for my current plight. Hell, any size would be perfect, who am I kidding? I think.

I leave the rope and blanket tangled and hang them on the winch near the hatch.

That was easy! I encourage myself. What's next?

I hoist myself up on the door frame to peer into the water and choose another target. It's hard to identify individual items among the confusion of things piled against the windows. Without my contact lens, everything is a blur unless it's a foot away.

I decide to try the feel test again, and lower myself until I feel the glass, then keep going. Some kind of fabric, then metal - a tool of some kind - then something soft. It must be a spare raincoat and sweatshirt, the ones on the seat. Useful. I grab with my toes again, trying for the soft sweatshirt. It lifts a few inches but then stops.

My toe switches to the raincoat, also stuck. I let go and hoist myself up so I can see into the water. Both are trapped under the fallen table. No hope. I was really lucky with the rope and blanket. Time to bite the bullet and look deeper.

I can see a few inches of air space in the main salon, just enough to let me breathe without moving outside the boat. I pull myself all the way in to the open hatch and study the chaos inside the cabin.

More plastic bags are floating, and I can see a half-gallon screw top plastic container - the kind I used to store pasta, flour, sugar, rice. It must be nearly empty to be bobbing around near the surface, but it's worth a grab. I make a mental note and resume assessing the bottom.

The vinyl roll is against the windows, its cardboard center disintegrating, but still compact. Another screw top container is nearby, this one clearly waterlogged. Most of the canned goods were stored behind the back of the settee and it is still lodged in place. It looked like the foam had swelled like a big sponge and it would be brutal to pull open.

I shift my attention to the galley, where the cupboards above the fridge are now horizontal and reachable like the windows in the pilothouse.

The sliding doors are only partly open, so it's worth a peek to see what's left. I wedge myself in the corner of the hatch, head up, and reach down into the galley with my feet.

I touch the cupboard door with my toes but it feels stuck in place. I can easily breathe so I try to wedge my foot into the small opening and shove the door open. Stuck. The thin wood is swollen in its track. I kick it, too light. Not much force in the water. I reach back and pretend the little door is a football. It cracks and leans inward. Another bump and it gives itself up.

**Page 117**

I decide the contents are worth a closer look so I take a big gulp of air and use the galley post to pull myself down to the shelf.   Mayo, mustard, salt, pepper, a glass jar of instant coffee and another of sugar. Halleluyah! Life is complete! I'm so excited I almost breathe in the water!

I pop to the surface and decide it's time to start collecting. I grab one of the floating grocery bags and pull myself down to the cabinet for the coffee, sugar and mayo. The mayo jar, half empty, tries to float but I put it in the bag with the rest and clasp it shut.

I rest a minute then take another breath and submerge for a closer look at the things that have settled on the settee back and the windows.

Before I surface I grab the vinyl and shove it toward the pilothouse. I reach up for another breath and I'm close to the floating container, so I add it to the bag. I can't spot the one that had sunk so I give it up and move back to the hatch for a rest.

I need more food so I wedge myself again to study the galley. I can't see any cans or the can opener. The bread maker is lying against the window and I try to peer inside the small cabinet. Something red. Funny shape. Jam! How did I miss the jam? Out of breath, you idiot.

What else did you miss?

The other slider is still in place, so I'll have to bash that in as well. I repeat my football move, successful the first time, then suck in as much air as I can and pull myself down to the cabinet. I push the pieces of door away and pull out a plastic baggy of elbow macaroni and a screw-top container of oatmeal. The rest of the cabinet was filled with spices and a completely sodden open bag of Oreos. Tragic.

I pop to the surface with my haul, which completely filled up my grocery bag. I tie it shut and head outside to secure it and take inventory. The vinyl roll is on the bottom, so I push it along with my feet to the doorway, then ease it halfway into the cockpit.

I give it a boost and grab the end. A couple of strings are keeping it in a roll, but saturated cardboard drifts away every time it moves. I dig my shoe out of my jacket and put it back on.

I have as much as I can swim with - maybe more - so I try to consolidate the blanket, the vinyl and the line in a bundle, and loop the tied grocery bag over my hand. I cushion the bundle under my chin, wrap my arms around my trusty fender and kick off.

The knife! I spin around and clamber back towards the doorway to retrieve the knife. I turn again and start kicking, but this time with the knife firmly clasped in my hand with the bag.

The soaked blanket and heavy rope slow my progress toward the shore but Raisin senses my return and sounds a loud bark. I head that way, and finally step onto the soft bottom. As I stand, water cascades out of the grocery bag and the blanket suddenly weighs 100 pounds. The saturated rope feels like it weighs twice that.

I drag them through the water until I reach the mangroves, then hoist them up on the branches to drain. I leave the fender there as well. I step carefully toward Raisin's occasional yelp, cradling the grocery bag, and plop down next to her wriggling body for a rest.

"How many days is it, Raisin?" I query my companion as she lays her head in my lap.

She had no good answer, just a blank look. No surprise there.

I try to assess the days that have passed since the storm began.

"I think it was August third or fourth that we were slammed, and the next day, too," I muse. "So I woke up on the beach on the fifth. Have we been in that camp for three nights or four? I can't believe I can't remember!"

# August 11, early afternoon

The first swim to 'Bama and the mud destroyed my squeaky clean feel, but it was worth it.

The sun is high overhead and I decide to risk another swim before going back to the camp. I get up and unwedge my cup of water. Nectar from the gods, for sure. I even share with Raisin. I rest for a few more minutes, give Raisin a big ear rub and stand up for my second round. I fasten the bag with the crook of a mangrove branch supporting the bottom and head out.

I'm still trying to puzzle out how much time has passed and resolve to make a record somewhere, marking a branch or some such.

I hoist myself up for another swim to the boat, zip up the jacket, cinch the waist, grab the fender and walk down the small rise and into the mucky water.

The swim gets easier every time, I think. The oil and diesel have almost dissipated so I can make a beeline to the boat, and I don't have to figure hand- and foot-holds.

"I'm a pro!" I mumble, kicking faster.

This time, I'm looking inside the head, I decide. From my familiar perch I can reach the hook that has kept the door from swinging open. With the boat on her right side, that door will flop wide open as soon as I release the hook. Whatever's inside will fall or float out towards the galley. I hope it's good!

Sure enough, a lot of things were floating. Half-empty vitamin and medicine bottles and other sealed containers and some baggies. A shampoo bottle slow-rolled its way out and down, and a near empty bottle of Palmolive dish soap bobbed up and down with the disturbance. Everything in the shower seemed wedged in place: spare towels, blankets, a plastic-wrapped case of paper towels. Mush. At the bottom, a bin and a milk crate of spares - toothpaste, soap, Tide, bleach, a bag of laundry clips, shampoo and conditioner. Contact lens solution! Wowza!

Yes!! I just need to get to it! I reach in and start dragging out and dropping what I can reach without going under, but it's not much. I hold myself in place with my elbows and reach with my legs and feet to pull out some more things, including the sodden paper towels. Heavy, even under water.

Finally, one bin is nearly clear so I gulp some air and sink far enough to wrap my fingers into the handhold. It's on its side, of course, so I need to twist it upright as I pull it out unless I want to chase its contents around the boat.

It takes three trips to the surface for air before I manage to lift it free but I'm beyond thrilled. I shuffle it outside and into the cockpit. As ecstatic as I am, I need to find some food.

I go back in and peer into the water for any sign of cans or a can opener, but no luck.

I eyeball the broken cupboard again, but nothing in there looks usable. I realize the heavy lid that covers the fridge and freezer is still in place. Maybe? It might be really disgusting and the minute that lid opens it will all come floating out. Worth the risk that something survived?

I remember the hunk of cheddar and log of salami that I'd put near the top to eat during the storm. That cheddar was pretty oily, I think. And salami has so many preservatives it lasts for years.

"Worth the risk," I say, steeling myself for the grossest thing I'll ever see. "It will get all over me," I shudder at the thought. But can it be worse than starving?

I delay the inevitable, sucking in deep breaths and shaking off my anticipatory nausea. Finally, I duck under the surface and reach down to grab the side of the broken cupboard. The fridge lid with its embedded pull rings, is vertical and there's very little room so I'll need to be almost on top of it when I open the lid.

I rise up for a breath now that I've scoped it out. It is what it is, I tell myself and sink back down. I yank on the pull ring and it budges a little but doesn't open. I pull on the other side - the freezer - and it's stuck, too.

I pop up, grab another breath and sink again, determined to succeed this time. Sure enough, two pulls and the heavy lid comes loose.

Not much happens… some brown leaves drift slowly up and the plastic bags inside shift position, but there is no explosion of old blood or rotted meat. Of course, those things are in the freezer side, and it's separate.

I float up for a breath then drop down again. The cheese is showing green spots, and so is the salami, but I shove them into my jacket, then move the sealed bags around. I spot some of those expired meat packets and grab those, but nothing else looks safe to eat. I shut the lid and pop to the surface for one more breath.

There has to be a can opener. I'm squinting over the spill on what is now the floor and spot an old beer can opener, from before pull tabs.

I grab it as my breath runs out, and rise up, gasping and tired. It goes inside my bathing suit, too precious to risk just inside the jacket.

"Great day!" I mutter. "Good job, even if I do say so myself!"

Silently, inside my head this time, I tell myself to shut up. "If someone hears," says my inner voice, "they'll know you're crazy, not just think it. Shut up!"

I reach the cockpit and consolidate my finds inside the milk crate. Except for the floaters, I think, and cram the sandwich meat packets inside my jacket.

I float on my back, resting from the strain and the fear, my eyes closed against the early afternoon sun. The sky is crayola blue, every last wisp of cloud banished, the best the Bahamas can be.

I stop my reverie and retrieve the crate. I tie the fender tightly across the top and hope the weight doesn't pull it under. I need the fender's help to get me to shore. I might need to winnow the load, save some for tomorrow.

Sure enough, the fender starts to lose the fight, so I lift the crate and study the contents.  I settle on the shampoo and conditioner, a bottle of Palmolive, and the food. The stuff in the bin can wait - two gallons of bleach, the other bottles of Palmolive, two half-gallons of vinegar. .

Suddenly, I have a manageable load and the fender floats nearly as high as it normally does. But I'll have soap, shampoo! I can brush my teeth, sort of! I give brief thought to looking for a hairbrush, but abandon it immediately. Tomorrow is another day.

I zip the jacket, hug the fender and push off the boat. The milk crate hangs near my belly.

It's slow going.

# August 11, afternoon

I follow Raisin's welcome back barks and struggle through the muck and up onto her little rise. I fend off her licks and untie the rope from her collar. She races into the water, stirring up the rotting leaves, then hurls herself back at me and gives me the pleasure of a generous shake. As if I'm not nasty enough.

I load the crate with my earlier findings and my sodden jacket. I manage to fold the roll of vinyl in as well. Heavy. Well, not heavy, exactly, about 15 pounds. But it's a slog and I'm tired. I'll dump what I can at the new camp, then go "home." Maybe sleeping at the new camp will have to wait until tomorrow.

"Come on! Home, James," I yell, not wasting time on a rest. I heft the crate and start off. I look at the angle of the sun. Probably around three, I think. No hope of making the closer camp tonight.

"But we'll have some real food, and a real bath and a real shampoo, right, Raisin?" She splashes ahead of me, paying no notice at all to my ravings.

We find a likely spot of wide beach 60 yards beyond the mangroves. The rocks are lower here, and the surf not as loud. It will do just fine. I settle the crate at the edge of the rocks and sort through what I'll take. The food, for sure, in case some other critter here is hungry. The soap - it can do double duty as shampoo - and conditioner to loosen the tangles. I've got the can opener - what did they used to call these? A church key! How fitting… I wonder why.

By now it's probably after 4, and we'll reach the camp in an hour, too late to get organized and come back. That's fine, I think. It's been a big day!

# ISLAND

# CHAPTER 54

# August 13, morning

I wake up thinking about the date.

I think it's been a week since I woke up on the island. I wonder what they named the storm. It's way down the alphabet from Hurricane Abysmal or Hurricane Monstrous. I wonder why they don't use words like that - build up people's vocabulary - instead of saccharine names like Betsy or Ian, when they're such brutal killers.

So I think the storm lasted three days, and I woke up here on the fourth. Have I been here a week? I can't remember. I've carved 10 lines into a sea grape trunk, but it might be 11. Maybe 12? Does it matter? Am I celebrating something or contemplating a long swim to nowhere?

"But you'd follow me out there, wouldn't you, Raisin? You would never let me swim by myself! You'd be badgering me with that tail, insisting I grab on!"

Raisin loved nothing better than acting as a lifeline with that strong tail… she'd tow me to China if I were inclined. When Jim and I explored together, a rare event, Raisin would be in constant motion swimming back and forth between us, whether it was five feet or 50.

"Nope, we can't have you swimming out into the deep deep, for sure." She wags twice more and sets off on her own excursions.

Yesterday I made a better sleeping arrangement and got more organized.

And eating! I ate half of the half of the peas that were left, and justified eating half of the soup by telling myself it would spoil. I don't think that is actually possible because of all the preservatives, but it eased my conscience. And I shared with Raisin.

The can opener did a great job - the can lid looked like something out of a monster movie with all those triangular holes, but it did the job.

Raisin chased down another green coconut for dessert, safer to eat with something else on my stomach.

I put the cheese and salami, the containers of pasta and oatmeal, the sandwich meat packets in a doubled plastic grocery bag and tied it into a shady tree to discourage the critters. The roll of vinyl wasn't big enough for much.

It could be a small roof, or a small waterproof ground cloth, but at six feet by 60 inches there wasn't enough fabric for both. For now, I opted for the ground cloth. I spent a couple of hours gathering up leaves as a base and laid the vinyl on top. It was a definite improvement to sleeping on my jacket.

I had spent at least an hour taking a soapy bath in the sea, washing my tangled hair, and repeatedly rinsing it with conditioner until I could actually run my fingers through it - most of the time - from the roots to the ends. After a final rinse, I plaited two Indian braids and sliced off smidgins of the vinyl to tie up the ends. With luck, the braids would keep future tangles to a minimum.

When I put my bathing suit back on, I could tell I must have lost some inches. Those days without food will do it, and the exercise, I think, pinching the suit's belly and feeling some slack.

My shorts are looser, too, with my whole hand fitting into the waistband.

# MIKE

# CHAPTER 55

## August 13, late afternoon

Mike hugged his beautiful daughter goodbye for the last time as she headed for the 12-seater at the small Great Harbour airport. Janet had spent her dad's first few vacation days with him, entrancing every man under 90 with her elegant walk and startling figure, on full display in her bikini.

"The fabric in that thing cost a thousand dollars a yard and you bought five dollars worth," Mike grumbled at her the first time she exited her cabin.

But he said it with a smile, amazed at having such a stunning offspring. Even better, he thought, she's happy, smart and knows just where she's going. Janet was in her third year of studying theatre, and had her eye on the Big Apple, New York.

She was going home for her junior year at the University of Michigan after spending her summer in summer stock. The Barn in Michigan offered up nine shows in three months, including seven musicals, Janet's passion.

Mike had managed his schedule so he saw her in three of the shows, two in leading roles. She'd been performing since grade school, starring in shows at a performing arts high school for four years.

Her voice and acting skills were second to none at UM, one of the best theatre arts programs in the country. She was headed for Broadway as soon as she graduated.

Mike was one proud papa. He wished the short vacation had been longer, but he was ready for some solitude.

The summer vacation he'd been planning had met with delay after delay, thanks to schedule changes, crew emergencies, other vacations, plus wanting to watch his girl at The Barn.

"Everything's a trade off," he muttered to himself. "The good part is that the water's nice and warm, not like April, so I won't catch my death from swimming all day."

He returned to the boat. He was alone for the first time in months. Countless hours of smiling at strangers, manhandling luggage, handing out drinks and dinners, solving problems took a toll.

And there were the strange beds, terrible schedules, never knowing the time, racing between flights, even the endless TSA lines…. He was ready for a stint of alone time, boring meals, no schedule. And the same bed two nights in a row.

"I'm a nomad," he tells new friends. He travels the world for American, the oceans in his Prout and the back roads in his camper.

He'd learned the hard way that his life was not amenable to long-term relationships. He'd missed too many birthdays and anniversaries due to late flights, bad weather, last-minute crew changes. And sometimes, more talking and smiling was the last thing he wanted when he got home. None of which led to a happy wife or girlfriend.

Thank goodness his kids didn't hold a grudge, he thought. They both loved to meet him for a few days of discovering far-off places as well as each other.

He tidied up the guest cabin and changed the sheets.

"You never know," he thought. "Maybe a mermaid will jump aboard. Or Cameron Diaz. But with long hair. And an allover tan.

"Or some damsel in distress. I'll rescue her, no strings attached! I'll be ready."

He jammed the sheets into a pillowcase for the coin laundry in the marina, straightened the coverlet and closed the door.

It was time for a book and a Kalik and a snooze before dinner. He settled into the cockpit and decided the afternoon breeze was perfect. The book slid to his chest and minutes later he was asleep.

# ISLAND

# CHAPTER 56

# August 14, morning

So this morning I'm clean, I'm organized, I'm closer to the boat and I have no excuse not to make a couple of trips for more supplies. I need to find more matches. The few I found after the rain were worthless.

What little of the red sparky part that remained after being submerged completely disappeared in the torrent. I'm crossing my fingers that I might find some surviving matches still in the boat. Or something else to make a fire.

The walk to the boat is nearly automatic now. Raisin climbs her little rise and dutifully awaits her leash. I still swim with my rain jacket for protection from the leaking diesel, and use the fender to help with the swim.

Small fish are starting to explore the inside of the boat, but scatter as soon as my feet disturb the hull. I'm braver about opening my eyes. It only stings for the first minute or two, then feels natural. I feel like I'm holding my breath better too. I'm not exploding up and gasping quite as often.

I'm thinking I need to retrieve that man overboard bag, the one that Jim complained was too heavy.

Well, it is too heavy, especially as it's waterlogged, but I reason that heavy things are lighter in the water. I'm going to try to pull it out.

The bag is resting partly in the bookshelf above the back of the settee. It must have bounced around during the worst of the storm, then settled when B'Ama fell on her side. That shelf and the settee back now constitute the floor of the boat. The trick will be to tie a solid knot through the handles of the bag and lift it out. There is so much line in the boat, I didn't bother to bring the piece I already retrieved.

After scoping out the bag, I return to the dinette and use my feet to pull out one of the skeins of rope resting on the windows. It's a decent size, half-inch, and plenty long. I take it to my cabin door handhold and undo it. I tie one end around the winch on the cabin top and unspool the rest until I get the other end, then swim back through the pilothouse. The rope cooperated nicely.

I take a big breath and pull myself down near the bag. I hang on with one hand and get the line through the handles on the first try, but run out of breath.

I push for the opening. The tide is higher today, leaving no air pocket in the cabin.  Next time I'll get the knot. But no go. I need both hands, and when I let go of my handhold, I'm a cork. Another breath. Ok, no knot this time. I'll just bring the end of the rope up with me, and snug it up from where I can breathe. Easier said than done.

I stand inside the cabin door and pull the rope tight but nothing budges. I fasten my end to the winch as well and move back inside the boat. When I peer into the water it's clear the bag is firmly wedged and needs to be jimmied out of its spot. Ugh. Am I ready for this? I wonder… if the bag weighs 50-plus pounds inland, what will it feel like underwater? I never did know that formula. Now I wish I'd learned it.

I take a really big gulp of air, then pull myself toward the bag with the doubled rope. I stand on the back of the settee - such an odd feeling - and pull on the handles of the bag. It gives a little then rolls a few inches away from the ledge that had held it. I jump up and back toward the doorway to get my breath before the next step. Now to pull it up, and not get it tangled into anything else.

I pull on the double rope and the bag actually slides across the settee back but doesn't want to climb the seat. I snug up the line on the winch and follow the rope again. This time, I stand on the drawer below the seat and hoist the bag up to clear the seat. It's not that heavy!

Another trip to breathe and pull the line again. This time the bag cooperates nearly to the two steps up to the pilothouse, then wedges between the head door and the galley wall. The bag is too wide and needs to pass through end-first.

I secure the line again, move as far into the hatch as I can and pull myself down. The last time? Please?

I reach the bag and turn it so it's pointing long ways and get it started up the steps. Done! I have to breathe. The next pull from the cabin door gets it almost within reach. Whoof, and up over the step and into the cockpit. I dunk headfirst to give it a lift. Not too bad… but how will I swim with it?

I'll figure that out after a rest, I think. I float on my back, letting my breathing slow to normal and enjoying the fact that my hair isn't floating around me like a cloud. A very ugly, tempestuous cloud.

I wonder about opening the bag here and being selective. I could set it on the hull. But as full of water as it is, I don't think I could lift it up. Could I drag it along the bottom? Maybe. But what if it rips open? Not good. One fender won't float it, but maybe two fenders could… worth a try.

I don't want to swim back empty-handed so I spend a few short dives gathering some more line, the floating plastic horn, some sealed plastic bags of mystery items, a metal plate and a kettle. Everything fits into one grocery bag, except the horn, so it was an easy swim back to shore.

Raisin's welcome directs me in and we head right back to camp to retrieve the second fender. I take the time to mix some oatmeal up in salt water and let it sit in the sun for a few minutes to "cook." I share with Raisin then slog back to her little mound. I tie her up and she settles in for a nap. I hang onto the rope of one fender and clutch the one that sacrificed its rope for a leash, and start kicking my way back to Wham B'Ama.

Once on board, I unwrap the lines from the winch and push one end through the center of the empty fender. It's like pushing fat spaghetti. It's a tight fit and the rope is reluctant to squeeze through the passage, but I'm persistent.

It's finally done and I pull the fender all the way down to the bag handle to see if it lifts. Not an inch. Crapola.

I tie the fender about three feet from the handles, and give the rope end a pull. The fender helps, for sure. I hoist it up onto the side of the boat.

In the water, it feels about 30 pounds. The question becomes how to rig the second fender. Do I risk attaching it as well? A disaster if the whole thing were to sink. Nope.

In the end, I retie the fender close to the handles and secure the other end of the rope to the winch. I let the bag go off the side of the boat, figuring were in a 10-foot hole. I'm right. I pull on the rope to check for buoyancy - none - and pull it up a couple of feet before lashing the second fender to the line. Halleluyah, it only sank a couple of inches.

It will be slow going, but I'll get that bag to shore. Maybe not to camp today, but I'll get it to shore!

I finish unwinding the rope from the winch, give 'Bama an adios, and slide into the water. I tuck the partly submerged fender under my chin, position the rope between my legs and slowly kick my way toward the island. Half way there, the bag hits bottom and I shorten the rope. Another 10 feet and I reach bottom, so I'm able to drag it.

I shorten the line for the last time, with the second fender keeping the bag off the bottom until it reaches my knees. Then I have to start dragging the full waterlogged weight over the muck and toward Raisin's occasional bark.


# August 14, afternoon

It takes everything I have to reach the muddy rise, dragging the bag inch by inch. With all the water inside, it must weigh at least 70 pounds, I think. And no point in trying to open it until I reach dry ground.

Finally! I sit on the bag to get my breath, strip off my jacket, and untie Raisin, happy to see me as always. She races off to explore something and I kneel in the mud to examine the bag's long zipper. It's covered by a fold of fabric, but its days underwater weren't kind. The pull-tab stubbornly stays in place.

Better leverage would help, I think, casting about for string or wire. The hoodie on my rain jacket ties with a string. I grab the plastic end and ease it out. Thankfully, it's not sewn in place, just snug.

I thread the end through the hole in the zipper pull. Doubled over, I have a nice long cord I can wrap around my hand and pull. Success!

As the zipper moves and the sides open, water spills out along with floating bits and pieces that look like treasure to me — a sealed bag of plastic bags, a floating container of waterproof matches, a floating battery lantern.

I rush to pull the sides of the bag together and control the flow, pulling out what I can see — a length of nylon cord, a plastic bag with a washcloth and bar of soap, a container of toothpicks, scissors, a sealed bag with a notepad, pencils, pens.

I start to gather things up in one end of the bag and dump the rest of the water out. I find sealed containers of protein bars, rice, pasta, bottled water, a hand-crank desalinator, cotton batting to start a fire, a signal mirror.

Raisin is back, examining the bounty, no doubt looking for something to eat. "I wasn't crazy, was I?" I query. "I don't care that the bag was too heavy… it's heavy with stuff that's going to keep us alive! Until some other idiot travels this far off the beaten path and decides to visit, like we did… but we won't die while we're waiting."

I gather up the bag's opening and tip it up to dump the remaining water. I've pulled enough out that I can easily lift it, but the shadows are getting long and I'm exhausted.

I put everything back in the bag except the container of energy bars — a feast! — a water bottle and the roll of cord. I close the zipper and use the cord to tie the bag handles to the mangrove.

"Is somebody going to come along and steal it? Really?" I laugh at my caution, then yell for Raisin.

I set off for camp with a lighter heart, cuddling the energy bars and water.

# August 14, late afternoon

The slog to the camp takes about an hour, and I resist the urge to sample my treasures. Good girl, I think. As usual, Raisin is bounding in and out of the water, nuzzling into piles of flotsam and seaweed, yapping at the odd crab, hunting for a coconut.

We reach our spot and I strip off my jacket and bathing suit, grab the soap and conditioner and make my way into deep water. Oh, the luxury… I float, arms out, legs barely moving, and bob in the gentle waves.

My hair streams out behind me, hardly any tangles, and I rouse myself to get clean. What joy to lather up, wash off the mud and leaves. I rub some conditioner into my hair and finger comb it, then dunk my head for a good rinse. I finish off with a short swim and walk ashore for a hearty supper.

Peeling the flimsy plastic wrapper from the energy bar is excruciating. I cup its folds and lick off every crumb. I torture myself and open a second bar, and do the same. At least seven peasized bits.

My first real bite is exquisite, spoiled only by Raisin's attack on my mouth. I move in time so her tongue grazes my cheek, but I get the message and break off a nibble for her. It vanishes.

We share the rest of the two bars - I get the lion's share, of course - then savor the pure water from the bottle. Raisin has to make do with rainwater. By now, the sun is at the horizon's edge and I secure the day's treasures and straighten my bed.

I'm still faintly hungry, but satisfied. Tomorrow I'll inventory all the food and try to divide it up. I know I'll be able to cook. I'll need to learn to catch fish. Tomorrow. Tomorrow.

Raisin curls up near my feet and we're asleep before the sky turns dark.

# ISLAND

# CHAPTER 57

# August 15, morning

I take a day off from swimming to 'Bama and instead lug the bag back to the camp. Sadly, I have to lug it through the mucky water at the edge of the mangroves, but it washes clean in the waves by the camp.

I drag it up 25 feet of sand so I can perch on a comfy rock and unzip it again. This time I hold the sides closed and control the emptying water.

I unroll one of the stiff, salt-crusted blankets, no good for much until a good rain rinse. But it's good for laying out the bag's contents. Matches, plastic bags, can openers, fish hooks, lures, spools of line, floating lantern.

I know I made mistakes. It wasn't waterproof, a big no-no. And it didn't float, which maybe is a good thing since it didn't float out of the boat.

Oh my gosh, the ditch bag is a lifesaver of the first order! Matches in a waterproof container, sealed bags of rice, pasta, a dozen cans of tuna. Condensed milk! I want to rip the can open with my teeth!

A weakness at the best of times, and this is light years away from that! But there are two can openers - the little Boy Scout one, and a regular crank one.

And of course fishing line, hooks, sinkers, a filleting knife, a rolled up plastic cutting board, a collapsible aluminum cup and bowl. The contents are a lifesaver for sure. Even a big bottle of aspirin, Betadine, Bandaids, a splint, Vaseline, Benadryl, Pepto Bismol.

"Raisin, I can get sick in a dozen ways and I have a cure," I shouted. She happily wagged that whip of a tail.

What else? A deck of plastic playing cards, as if I would ever get bored here! Two of those silver NASA blankets that look like aluminum foil but actually work to keep me warm or cool, whichever's needed. And dry.

Survival food like cookies, tins of treats like gum and chocolate, some basic tools, knives, razor knife, a saw.

Even seeds! Lettuce, radish, spinach, squash, tomatoes, melons. The problem would be finding the dirt to plant them in. A hand-crank desalinator.

Oh! The muscles I'm growing with that thing! But with the rain only intermittent - a mixed blessing - it's a lifesaver.

I think of Lupe and her foraging lessons every time I look at the sparse plants on this little island, crossing my fingers that I won't have to remember which I can eat. If I'm careful, I could last for years without having to forage. Maybe.

# ISLAND

# CHAPTER 58

# August 16, morning

My project now that I'm well supplied is dog food for Raisin. I have high hopes that the industrial trash bags the dog food is wrapped in might have survived. One bag, that I'd pulled out of the locker just before the storm, was still wedged on the floor of the V-berth where I'd left it.

It's in the deepest, furthest part of the boat and I only have a few seconds to work before I have to surface to breathe. I'm equipped now with my snorkel and mask, retrieved from the cockpit locker. But even though I can see well, I still can't hold my breath for long.

In the first dive I swim in and down, confident compared to the early days. I put my feet on each side of the V-berth doorway, bend down and pull on a corner of the bag. It moves maybe an inch, but the industrial black bag is strong and doesn't even stretch.

I try again. And again. In an hour of repeated dives, I manage to move the bag a foot away from its resting place. And I'm beat. Tomorrow is another day.

I reach the cockpit and relax against the familiar doorway. I know the boat better now than I ever did when we were sailing her.

I've probed every hole, every locker, every cupboard. And god knows I've shed many a tear over her. But she saved me, tossing me to safety even while she suffered her own death throes.

I tap the cabin top and give the beautiful curve a stroke. "You're a great boat, 'Bama. I'll love you forever," I murmur.

Raisin has sensed my work is done for the day and I hear her bark calling me home. She's learned she can't come to the boat so she's not tied anymore, but waits patiently in chest-deep water. She knows I might return with a treat. On one trip I found a big plastic container of Milk Bones. She got one a day until they were gone, but - like all dogs - hope springs eternal that more will materialize.

# ISLAND
# CHAPTER 59
# August 17, morning

I'm determined to rescue the bag of dog food. I swim with every floating device I've rescued to 'Bama's side and muscle them into the boat. One by one, dive after dive, I manage to tie them to the dog food bag and lash a sturdy line around the middle. I have to be careful because I don't want the plastic to rip, so I protect the bag with some towels.

Sure enough, the floats lift the bag just enough so I can maneuver it easily through the main salon to the steps. Then I need to shorten the lines because the water is shallower, but I was closer to my air supply so it went quickly.

Up the steps and out to the cockpit, then a quick bowline around the line to shore and I'm set. I step off the boat and start pushing my prize toward the mangroves. Raisin will dine like a king tonight!

# MIKE

# CHAPTER 60

# August 24

Mike finally pulled himself away from Grand Harbour. He'd been enjoying the limited nightlife and readying the boat again for a long cruise, giving everything a good fresh-water wash and topping up his tanks. Double-checking the systems.

He'd also been making calls, and managed to wangle another month off, so he didn't have to be back in the sky until after Thanksgiving. That was a real coup!

But he had friends who owed him, and he was calling in the chits… all those flights he'd taken so they could celebrate birthdays or go to school plays. It finally paid off.

"I'll make it all the way to the end of the chain this time," he told his daughter in their weekly call. "I'll be out of touch for a while, so don't worry. It might even be a couple of months."

Mike was excited about the trip. He had mixed feelings about it being a solo voyage. He was past ready for a break from people, and he was between girlfriends. He was happy to be alone but he didn't want to be lonely.

His work schedule - coupled with jealousy of all the nights he spent with other crew - spelled doom for every woman he'd been with. His second marriage lasted the longest and produced his two great kids, but in the end his wife suspected affairs and hated that he was never around for birthdays or anniversaries.

And, he knew, she was aware he still carried a torch for his first wife, his high school sweetheart. Katy was his first love and his last girlfriend, as well. They'd rekindled the flames on land in the last year, but as soon as she was on the boat, everything disintegrated. She didn't want to sail, hated the motion of the boat in the sea, refused to learn to steer, took long showers and used up all the water. It was a disaster.

Mike labored over the decision to end it, or to give up his sailing dreams, swallow the anchor, as they say, and spend all his time ashore to be with Katy.

But he started sailing as a kid and never stopped. It renewed him, made him feel whole. Alone in an anchorage, diving for his dinner, sipping a rum in the cockpit as the sunset's colors exploded over the water… he never felt more alive. As much as he loved Katy, he loved being on the water more. So here he was, alone.

"It's good," he said to himself. He untied the last line from the dock, and motored slowly out of the harbor.

He set the autopilot and tidied up as the boat steered itself toward the deep water. He removed the fenders and stowed them in the cockpit locker, along with the dock lines and the winch covers. The sails were already rigged, so he went forward to untie the main and the jib sails.

He looked around to make sure there were no hazards, and pointed the boat into the wind, resetting the autopilot. He hopped back up on the cabin and cranked the main up, watching it flap lazily in the light wind. Then he went to the other side of the mast and raised the jib. The jib sheets - the lines that ran from the bottom corner of the sail to the cockpit - ran free and he raced back to the cockpit to snug it up. He snapped off the autopilot and tightened the main sheet until the big sail filled. He felt the boat surge forward under the power of the wind, stopped the engine, corrected his course and breathed a sigh of relief. "I'm gone," he thought. "I'm free!"

# ISLAND

## CHAPTER 61

## August 24, afternoon

The days start to run together. Every day I make another mark on my calendar tree, eat leftovers for breakfast and make my way to 'Bama to salvage some more goodies or just watch the schools of tiny fish that have set up camp inside the hull.

After establishing the new camp and rescuing some basics, I rigged a long line from the boat to a sturdy mangrove on the shore. So instead of swimming, I can just pull myself hand over hand to the boat. The line also lets me suspend my findings in a milk crate or canvas bag for the trip to shore.

The bathroom's contents were life-changing.

The medicine cabinet and the cabinet below the sink were both still closed with hooks, so I knew I hit the jackpot. The problem was that they were now basically the roof. When I undid the hooks everything would fall out.

I needed to position a big bag around each door to catch the contents. Inside the medicine cabinet were spare contact lenses and solution, eyeglasses, toothbrush and toothpaste, hairbrush, razors, everything I used every day and never gave a thought to.

Makeup! Not that I ever used it.

The cabinet under the sink held Dawn, a scrub brush, scrubby sponges, more lens solution. I could see with two clean contact lenses! I was ecstatic.

It took many days to rescue the food on board, but for once I was grateful I was a bit of a hoarder when it came to basics. I had enough canned tomatoes to feed an army, corned beef hash, corn, canned roast beef and chicken, tuna, black beans, even small potatoes. For dessert I had cans of pineapple, mixed fruit, condensed milk.

I even found a stash of long-forgotten long-life milk in cartons that had survived the abuse of the storm. And jars of instant coffee! Halleluyah! My life was complete! There was a celebration that day!

I tried to keep the labels from totally disintegrating, but they were waterlogged. And moving them around didn't help, so I did my best to keep them in groups - meats, fruits, veggies.

Eating would be a crap shoot, but at least I'd be eating!

For staples, I managed to save some double-bagged flour and sugar, as well as a couple bags of cereal. The boxes had softened and washed away but the plastic bags inside didn't leak. I retrieved bags of beans, even the wet ones, to dry out again, or cook.

I gave up on retrieving my favorite cast iron Copco pans that I'd bought in college. Gorgeous and indestructible but heavier than a dead preacher, as my best friend would put it. She was right. Each one could be an anchor on its own. So I opted for the two throwaway pans I collected the first day. They did the job.

# MIKE

# CHAPTER 62

# August 24

This first day was a short one. Right now he was just sailing for fun, no destination. He could stop in Nassau, but did he want the hustle and bustle? All those cruise ships? Nope.

Eleuthera has the most beautiful water, everybody tells him that… better choice. He relished the sound of the waves agains the hull and spotted a pod of dolphins off the bow.

He activated the autopilot again and grabbed his camera for some pictures of their antics. As he sat on the bow, the dolphins blew saltwater on him and squeaked their joy in this glorious day. "I'll squeak too," he thought. "I'm at least as happy as they are!"

The hours passed and he could make out Eleuthera in the distance. He'd pull in close for protection and enjoy a quiet first night.

It took another two hours and the sun was low in the sky when he nestled the boat into a small cove for the night. He dropped and tidied the sails, and watched the bottom for a nice sandy spot for the anchor.

Not too close, no coral heads, no seaweed… he dropped the anchor and coasted to a stop, then reversed the engine to make sure it was set.

"Nothing worse than that sound of a dragging anchor at 3 a.m.," he muttered.

He was just in time to watch the evening panorama of color. He ate his dinner of a grilled cheese sandwich and tomato soup as a three-quarter moon rose in the east, throwing a silver path across the water.

The morning came early and Mike woke himself up, dreaming of a quick dive overboard. He clipped the slim floating safety line to the belt loop on his trunks. Despite what many thought of as a daredevil lifestyle, jet-setting around the world for decades now, Mike was the voice of caution.

That was another issue he'd had with Katy. More than once, she'd dived into the water while he was busy, then yelled for help in a panic because she was drifting away. She didn't listen, wasn't safe. Scary to have around. So she's not.

All pilots - and anyone around them - knows the rubric, There are old pilots and bold pilots, but there are no old, bold pilots!

Even the most seasoned sailors have been swept away, mostly men as they pee off the stern. A few years before, the famous sloop owned by a woman who'd circumnavigated and written books about her adventures was found empty off West End.

It was assumed she'd gone for a swim and had been caught in the deadly current and was never able to get back to her boat.

Mike took all the lessons to heart and never went into the water without a tether even though he could swim like a fish. So could all those others whose empty boats had been found.

# ISLAND
# CHAPTER 63
# September 3

I'd rescued my mask and snorkel out of the cockpit locker in one of my last forays to scavenge the boat. Getting those lockers open was a bear. Water had leaked into the plywood and it had swelled.

The locker on the high side of the boat was easier to work on because I could actually breathe while I did it. I had a couple of long, fat screwdrivers so I just chipped away at the sides of the lid until I could lift it. All the dive and snorkel gear was in there, along with spare ropes, fenders for 'Bama, a bag of small driftwood.

Once I had my mask and snorkel I spent hours in the water enjoying the sights, as well as continuing my salvage work.

The little bay was so protected I didn't worry about any currents, but I'd swim with a long floating line with a small anchor on the end. If I ever got caught, I'd be able to stop myself from being carried away.

As I swim out from the beach, I spot the starfish that's been slowly making her way south for the last week and a spectacular tellin, one of my very favorites, with a delicate shell like a rainbow. She is sitting upright, shell open to catch some food. As I disturb the water with my fin, she yanks her shell closed and sinks into the sand.

I've been watching the subtle changes below as fall sets in and days are shorter. Earlier in the summer I watched with amazement as conchs mated… they stayed locked together for days.

Then I saw the magic of the emergence of egg sacks. Every sea creature's was different. The conch spent two weeks laying a fat brown tube. The one I saw was more than a foot long.

The mother conch finally moved away, leaving the casing to lie quietly in the sand until the microscopic eggs transformed into perfect tiny conchs. The tube consisted of hundreds of tiny compartments like a honeycomb. When they hatched, smaller than a grain of sand, they left the sack to float off in the tide.

I'd find dried egg sacks on the beach after a storm, sad victims of a poor choice by their mom, but a scientific marvel to me.

I could shake the tiny creatures into my hand and examine them under a loupe. (Yet another crazy thing I'd put in the ditch bag!) I'd peer through the lens to see a perfect miniature creature - a tiny queen conch, a horse conch, a turban, tulip, triton. Each tiny shell was encased in its own small space - like a honeycomb - and each kind of shell produced a distinctive egg sack shape.

It almost makes me believe. I'd think every time I found another, how else could such profound perfection have started?

I spent hours examining the bay and befriending the creatures whose home it was. A big green turtle always knew when I entered the water and would lure me into the deep. He was a much better swimmer, and would stay 20 feet ahead, twisting and turning, casting glances over his shoulder to make sure I was following. Sometimes he'd swim a circle around me and taunt me to grab his shell. I'd never hang on, but I'd run a hand over his slimey back. He became a fast friend.

Another, even friendlier, was a stingray. He must have had a greater range than the turtle, because he would disappear for days at a time. But when he returned, we reveled in each other's presence. He'd swim close and let me stroke his back, then dash off and wait for me to follow, then return again. It was the ray's version of tag, I think. He reminded me of my second husband, mercurial.

Scarier were the barracuda that sometimes peered at me as I swam back and forth from the boat or just drifted, sight-seeing. There were two, never together, but one distinctly bigger at about four feet.

He would appear in a flash as I started my swim back to shore, hovering just out of reach, mouth agape to show his terrifying teeth. His shiny gray eyes drilled into mine.

I'd swim with my head cocked to watch him,  conquering my wish to levitate and fly to shore. Most times, he'd amble away as I reached shallow water and stood up, but sometimes I'd be halfway to shore and he'd disappear so fast I didn't even see it, even though I was watching.

Those times were terrifying. Those times, I'd drop my legs vertical and spin, looking for him. Nothing. A few strokes and I'd look again, head underwater, breath catching in fear.

Barracudas are stealth killers, biters. I'd seen barracuda scars on arms and legs and it was never a pretty sight - a massive jagged scar deep into the flesh. I was always amazed the victim hadn't bled out. So I was scared. If he decided I was a snack, I'd be done for.

On the beach, I spent hours watching a community of hermit crabs. I'd lay out some tiny leftovers to coach them out of their holes. Once out, they would perform their endless inspection of other shells that might prove more comfortable.

Sometimes, a hermit crab would take a liking to a shell already occupied and would climb on top, hanging on for dear life and making life miserable for his captive. One or the other would give up. If it was the captive, he would only have minutes to find another shell - maybe that of his tormenter - or meet certain death from the sun or another predator.

One thing about the hermits, though, was their predictability. If a crab liked a certain spot on a certain branch, no number of shell changes could mask his identity. They were like people that way, I thought… or the Aesop's fable about the leopard.

# CHAPTER 64

# September 20, afternoon

As the days, then weeks, passed, Raisin and I settled into a routine. The calendar tree had lots of slashes now.

Being a writer all my life, I had always communicated better with a typewriter or laptop. The cloak of being a writer let me approach people, ask questions, talk for hours.

But in social situations I was often tongue-tied, as shy as when I was a child. On the island I often wished for a huge pad of paper and endless supplies of pens, but the gods were not that kind. What paper I found was in shreds, even the bagged up logbook in the emergency bag.

So I was talking out loud more than I ever had in my life. My audience, Raisin, was thrilled and only rarely fell asleep in the middle of a story. I was enjoying recalling my crazy life, crazier boyfriends and how I ended up on this island. I'd settle onto my "story rock," a nice concave stone with a big fallen limb behind it.

"Maybe Travis McGee will rescue me, eh? I've been waiting decades for that guy! It's about time he shows up!'

Raisin obligingly lays her head on my lap.

"So how on earth did I end up on boats?

"Going back to the very beginning, when I lived in San Francisco I dated a guy, Rick, who had a Thunderbird, a very spare 28-foot plywood boat," I began. "He loved to race, so I was crew every Wednesday night, Saturdays and Sundays for months.

"We raced his boat, or helped a friend on his 30-footer. Racing in San Francisco Bay was always exciting - cold, foggy, always windy. Death defying. Once, we were returning from a race and got caught in an outgoing tide. Sailing for all we were worth, with the engine at full speed, we were steadily moving backwards under the Golden Gate Bridge. Not auspicious.

"He was cute and fun, but a hopeless alcoholic. We were once asked to leave the very posh St. Frances Yacht Club for necking at the bar. I fell in love with sailing, but not him.

"It was just a few years later that I answered that ad in Cruising World." I paused. I had a confession to make.

"Raisin, when I was there, I had another doggie, because you weren't here yet.

"His name was Bilbo and he was a collie born on the Navajo reservation in Arizona. He was a beautiful dog, and you would have loved him, just as I did.

"He was an adventurer, too, and once fell out of my seventh floor apartment window because he tried to chase a bird. A lady on the third floor saw him go by her window and left a note on my door that she had him.

"But don't worry," I told Raisin. "He landed in some bushes and wasn't even hurt."

Back to the ad, I tell myself. Raisin doesn't want to hear about my doggie baggage.

"In the distant pre-history, before the internet, before cell phones, there were magazines. And people would run ads in magazines to meet other people. Like Match-dot-com, but much slower.

"I never should have written that letter… but we've had so much fun since, eh?

"I even remember parts of what it said…

*"I am presently a land-locked woman working in Phoenix while I save for an around-the-world voyage…*

"Oh, Raisin, how naive I was  then!

"I'm so lucky to make it to the Bahamas all these years later, and it's been heaven on earth. Who needs anything more?

*"I am a voracious reader. My favorite authors can turn a phrase as well as tell a tale - Steinbeck, London, Graham Greene, John D. McDonald. I want my very own Travis McGee."*

"Oh, Raisin, how many potential Travis McGees I got to know, all disappointing. A couple were close, but not close enough, eh? Chip Shaw could have been a keeper. It was never Jim or a dozen others. No judgments, kiddo," I urged. "I've had a great life, mostly single! And you, my lady, are a bitch so don't complain."

That flagpole of a tail was on full alert. I resumed telling her about the letter to *Arlen, the one that changed my life.*

*"I can't put down anything written about the sea or sailing or sea creatures. Water comforts and renews me, even if I'm reduced to floating in a lake in a*

*rubber raft. I loathe swimming pools, just as I hate preservatives in food, polyester clothing, fake coffee 'cream' and plastic in almost any form.*

"Well, all of that is still true, isn't it, Raisin?

"I'd still rather scrub a deck than a floor, and I still take great joy in varnishing and working with wood. I wonder why. I just wish I had a deck to scrub right now, right? Come on, enough of these crazy memories, let's go for a swim!"

Raisin bounds up and into the water before I can stand. I may still love to varnish, I think, but these creaky knees came from all those hours of kneeling on the deck.

I walk down the beach and into the water deep enough to float. My braided hair tickles my shoulders and I survey my all-over tan. I gave up the bathing suit weeks past, saving it for a rainy day or a rescue, whichever comes first.

For the first time since my second divorce (don't let me start) I can see my ribs. I'm almost the color of the ripe coconuts we're still eating and I chuckle at my lifelong mantra: Brown fat is so much more attractive than white fat. No fat now, I think. My shorts that were snug are falling off. I've dropped 20 pounds at least, and feel great.

# ISLAND

# CHAPTER 65

## September 20, evening

As Raisin gulps her share of dinner, I think again about how I got here.
What else did I tell Arlen?

*"Sailing is my heart's delight... I love the hard work that comes with it. I love the sound, the smells, the movement, the demands of the sea. I'm not afraid of the water or the waves or of storms.* (Little did I know when I wrote that line!) *I react well in a crisis and think clearly in times of stress."*

There's another shocker, I think.

Should I have quit while I was ahead? Naaah. Even this, this island, this solitude, I wouldn't miss for the world. If no one ever comes, I will have lived.

"Raisin, if they're coming, I hope they come before the food runs out, right? I really don't want to try to remember Lupe's lessons! And you'll have to learn how to catch fish! Not just chase them!"

Her tail wags in sympathy and I stand up to ready our bed for the night.

By now it's pretty comfortable.

I had retrieved the solid foam cockpit cushions from the boat and gave them a good freshwater rinse. Side by side, the cushions make a nice wide bed, and I keep the two pieces fastened together with some lengths of parachute cord. I couldn't rescue a pillow but I've learned to sleep without one.

The nights are getting chilly - it's nearly October after all - so the emergency blanket does a great job of keeping me warm, along with Raisin's snuggles. I wish enough rain would come to really rinse the fuzzy blankets. They're surface dry now, but still gummy from the salt.

The cursed awning and poles turned out to be a blessing. The poles were long enough to cut in pieces to make a teepee shape. It took some days to lash them together and spread the poles out so they didn't fall over, but I managed. The awning was big enough to cover most of the outside. The tiny foresail - the only one small enough for me to drag through the water - covered what the awning didn't reach. I was so glad I paid attention to those western movies.

Like the Indians, the opening faced east and I thanked the spirits every day I woke up. The teepee let me stay on the beach rather than force me into a lean-to using the mangroves. The mosquitoes would have eaten me alive.

As we walk our evening beach patrol, I keep a sharp eye on the horizon. It's been a clear, cloudless day, prime for seeing a green flash. As the sun touches the horizon, I perch on a rock and stare, unblinking, as it sinks.

"BAM! There it was!" I shout at my only audience. "Raisin, did you see that? We'll have to put our special mark on the calendar tree! That makes four! And people think it's a myth… but we know better, eh, kiddo?"

Walking back to the teepee, I wonder for the hundredth time what had happened to Jim.

In the weeks I'd been here, I'd crisscrossed the island and fought my way through the mangroves to find any sign of him. There was nothing to show he had made it ashore. I could only think he had left the boat — willingly or by the force of the wind and the waves — and had been swept out to sea.

# MIKE

## CHAPTER 66

## September 20

"Eleuthera is as spectacular as everyone said," Mike was writing a letter to his daughter as he waited for the sun to drop below the horizon. He was determined to see the green flash on this trip, and it demanded total concentration to catch it.

"I'm pulling out tomorrow for parts unknown… unknown by me, at least. You would love it here! Reefs, fish, pink sand, terrific restaurants. It's been easy to anchor anywhere and dinghy ashore. One beach has an abandoned Club Med that was fun to explore, and the pink beach there was nearly a mile long.

"I stocked up on books in Governor's Harbour, a destination for people from all over the world. Needless to say, I fit right in. The yachties all trade books, and they're nearly all about some crazy sailor or other. Like me.

"I picked up a dozen or so by a writer I never heard of, John D. McDonald. The paperbacks are pretty old, but I like the way the guy thinks. One book is a pretty accurate story about some idiots in Florida who ignore hurricane warnings and have a party in their condo instead. Terrific!

"I have a few more to read and the hero is a private eye type  who lives on a houseboat in Fort Lauderdale. He won the boat in a poker game so he calls it the Busted Flush. He's an interesting character, reminds me a bit of myself. He's a real straight-arrow, although at first glance you'd never think it. And he's always helping maidens in distress.

"Anyway, honey, I'm writing you this because I can get bad internet here and no phone service. I love you and you know I'll write or call when I can. Love, Dad."

Mike tucked his notebook away and looked at the sky.

"Damn, I missed it again!" He smacked his forehead in frustration. He'd seen the flash once before so he knew it was for real, and he just had to prove to himself he hadn't imagined it.

The green flash was one of the few things he hadn't checked off his bucket list. After 30 years flying every international route there was, he'd seen glaciers, northern lights, the Great Wall, kangaroos and koalas, Table Mountain, the Berlin Wall, wild elephants, the Taj Mahal. Name a famous place and he'd been there, done that. More than once.

And as much as he still loved the travel, he regretted that he had rarely shared his adventures with someone he loved. He would like to look across the table and say, "Remember that crazy guide we had in Kathmandu?" Or "I loved the Sea of Cortez! How many whales did we see that one day?"

As it was, he had a thousand memories with a thousand different people, some who'd been friends for years, but many more who were friends for a day or a week or a month. That's why he pined for Katy. They had memories they shared.

The trouble was, he wanted to share those memories across a table in the cockpit, waiting for the green flash, or cuddled in the big dinette enjoying a lobster that had been hiding under a rock two hours before. And Katy would never be that person.

The person he wanted would be comfortable running naked on a beach or swimming with the turtles. She'd love the wildlife as much as he did, able to spend hours watching the hermit crabs or tracking the sunset to spot the green flash. She'd be as happy with the disasters - and there were always disasters - as the pleasures, and she'd happily make the best of whatever came her way.

That sure wasn't Katy, who needed everything perfect all the time… and it hadn't been any of the women who'd joined him on his boat so far. None could imagine a life without makeup, for a start. Or bottles of sunscreen!

# MIKE

## CHAPTER 67

## September 21

Mike rose early and had the anchor up before the sun. He turned on the autopilot and motored slowly along the edge of the island. As he waited for a good signal so he could send his letter, he sluiced the deck with the saltwater pump, washing away the sand and footprints from his week's stay.

He'd stop for the night at Exuma, really popular with cruisers in winter, then mosey on to Cat Cay, a pretty short hop.

As the sun rose to turn the sky Crayola blue, he felt a hint of a breeze tickle his neck.

"Yes! A spinnaker run!" He smiled to himself.

Tricky for a single hander, but the boat was rigged for it and he loved the thought of that huge multi-colored sail leading him south. He set the autopilot to steer with the wind and ran through the complex tasks to safely raise the huge sail without dropping it into the water or getting it tangled up in the rigging.

"Done!" Mike flipped off the autopilot and took the wheel, raising his coffee mug in a toast. The boat surged through the slight swell, lifting with the power of the spectacular sail. Mike stood with spread legs, checking the compass and seeing he was on a perfect heading for his next stop.

# ISLAND

# CHAPTER 68

# September 23

Despite my solitude, I'm really happy.

I'd be rescued or I wouldn't. I'd see a passing boat and be able to signal them or I wouldn't. I'm ready for that. I have a signal mirror, a fire, a wet blanket to make smoke.

I fastened a couple of sheets onto the mangroves. I even have an air horn that works sometimes. But worrying or being scared won't change a thing.

My teepee keeps me feeling cozy and safe overnight and protected from the occasional rain. My fire pit is great for cooking and I manage a decent meal every day, even if it's rice and beans.

Raisin has many months of dog food and she always shares my leftovers.

I don't miss people or tv or the phone. Somebody out there might be wondering what happened to me, but I can't worry about that either. The constant evolving magic of the natural world entrances me every day.

I have so much time to think about my life, all the good and bad decisions that got me here.

Demanding guys, cheating guys, drunk guys, the occasional terrific guy… I think I might finally know what I want in the right guy.

I want him to be happy with me, that's all, and to make me laugh. But happy with me: grouchy in the morning, tousle-haired, curious, spontaneous, quick-tempered and tolerant both, honest to a fault, a night owl of the first order.

I want a guy who'll sneak up behind me while I'm washing the dishes and grab my ass, who lets me know in no uncertain terms that I turn him on.

"Do people still say that, Raisin, or do they just say he wants sex?

"I don't know, I like my way better. If all he wants is sex, he can get a blow-up doll. If he wants me, I'm ready."

But right now Raisin is my ideal partner.

She's always ready for an adventure, never complains about how I look, loves everything I cook. Great conversationalist! What more could I possibly want? Well, great sex. But she has two counts against her - a girl and a dog.

# CHAPTER 69
# September 23

Cat Island, yet another set of unrivaled beaches and glorious reefs. It boasted the tallest spot in all the Bahamas, a 200-plus foot stone turret, part of an old monastery. Cat also claimed a pit stop from Christopher Columbus, although there was no proof. Ok, Mike thought. But I'm here for the water... I think I'll pass on the turret and the marker.

He chuckled remembering a series of photos a cruising friend of his showed. The first photo showed Martin lying in a hammock in the cockpit of his boat with a low island with palms and mangroves in the background.

Martin held a handwritten sign that said "Cat Island."

In the next picture, very similar, he held a sign that said "Great Inagua."

In the third picture, this time on the opposite side of the hammock but another wooded island behind him, "Rum Cay."

By the time his sign said "Crooked Island," the jig was up. It was always the same island. Only the signs changed.

The point was that every one of the 700-plus islands had a LOT of similarities - a beach, mangroves, palms, pines on the sound side and big rocks and maybe a beach on the ocean side.

All but 30 of the islands were uninhabited, leaving cruisers to pick their personal favorite at their leisure.

Mike was determined to find that favorite on this trip. He had at least 680 islands to go. He loved pulling up close to an island with no other boats in sight and walking the beach, knowing his footsteps might be the only ones there for a year or 10 years.

He'd watch the ghost crabs, taunt the hermit crabs with bits of meat, fight through the brush to see the ocean side and find some washed up treasure.

To him, every one of these islands had its own charm. One might be a nursery for sharks, another might be a rookery for some small bird or other.

He'd walk along the rocks and spot the tiny speckled eggs laid in the small indentations.

"I should at least have a dog," he muttered to himself. "As it is, I'm talking to myself out here… that's pretty scary. My boss would make me see a shrink if she knew. If I had a dog, I'd have an excuse to be talking out loud about all this stuff."

He chuckled. "Maybe I could borrow a dog for my next trip. Or a parrot. He could talk back!"

# MIKE

## CHAPTER 70

## October 12

After 10 weeks, Mike is finally nearing the southernmost islands of the Bahama chain.

'I've made a big dent in seeing those 670 uninhabited islands, but my friend was right… they do start to all look the same,' he thought, nursing a Kalik as the boat drifted over starfish and lemon sharks near Crooked Island.

He'd dodged back and forth between the eastern and western island groups, Andros, Exuma, San Salvador, depending on where the wind was taking him. The tiny islands were the best, the ones with no names where no one may have stopped for years.

The beach junk fascinated him, but he was selective about what he kept: a hand carved wooden head that looked like Nefertiti, a huge turtle head left in a bush for the bugs to clean, a square brown bottle from Africa.

On one island he found a piece of a rocket engine. It was too big and heavy to lift, but he took a picture and made a drawing of where it was to send to NASA when he got back.

Now he was ready to round Acklins and jump into the open Atlantic for his return trip. His chart showed an isolated island that he wanted to explore. The tiny island showed a tricky entrance to the anchorage, but his boat's shallow draft just laughed at most obstacles.

Samana was 60 miles from any other land and had never been occupied. Just right. The reef should be spectacular and the lobsters ought to be tame enough to crawl right out of their holes.

He spent the next couple of days anchored near the southern end of Acklins, restocking and tidying the boat from his weeks of idling along in calm water. He called his daughter to catch up with her and emailed her all the letters he'd been writing.

He topped up his diesel and water in case he decided to stay outside - in the ocean - after he visited Samana. He had a month to get back to the boat's home port in the Berries and just a week after that to strip her down and get back to work.

'Hell, it'll take a week to shave and get a haircut,' he pulled on the beard he hadn't trimmed during the trip, normally very tidy and short.

His hair was another story. Ok, so his forehead was a little broader than it used to be, but now his dishwater blonde locks could only be called wild and woolly. Nevertheless, when he threw on a shirt and went ashore, he still felt appraising eyes from the women he passed. He was hazelnut brown and had lost his extra 15 pounds in the last few weeks. He almost had a six-pack, thanks to all the diving and exploring.

When he went into a beach bar for a cold beer and some conversation, he could have his pick of women. He'd had his pick all his life, from passengers in the first class cabins he served to wealthy and beautiful women who lived in the world capitals he visited on a regular basis. Not to mention his fellow cabin attendants, all slim and gorgeous and young. And in the same hotel.

'I've had enough one nighters and Miss Right Nows,' he thought to himself, shrugging off the advances of an exotic 20-something at the bar.

'I'm finally grown up enough for a real woman who wants the real me, warts and all,' Mike mused, 'missed birthdays, weird schedules. A sailor. Somebody who laughs at my jokes and wants to hear my stories. Somebody who has a sense of humor, whose disasters turn into funny stories.

'Somebody who can spend an hour watching a hermit crab change his shell, or go for a dive or raise the sails or chart our next stop. Or make love in the sand. Or the cockpit. Every day. Someone who wants this life as much as I do. Tall order.'

# ISLAND
## CHAPTER 71
## October 15, morning

Like every other day this week, the sun streams into the opening of my teepee and smacks me right in the face. No sleeping in today. "Raisin, why didn't you block that sun for me? Let me sleep, eh?" She peers out of the opening, her wagging tail barely missing my face.

As I crawl up and out, she launches herself across the sand and into the water. I follow her and dunk my head, then go ashore for the shampoo and soap.

Washing my hair and gathering it into a controllable mass makes me feel human, civilized. I don't care that I'm spending my days like a naked monkey, practically swinging through the trees. The trees I swing through are all underwater, but the incentive is the same… curiosity and fun.

After my dip, I shake the sand out of the fuzzy blanket on my flat rock armchair and grab the bowl of dinner leftovers. Last night's feast included corned beef hash - a no-label surprise - with pinto beans and canned peas. I savored my one daily cup of coffee - cold, slightly salty, with sugar. Nectar of the gods.

Desserts are a distant memory. A half-dozen cans of pineapple and mixed fruit, a couple of jars of jam, three cans of condensed milk. All gone.

I'd been a glutton, in part because the cans were recognizable even with the labels washed away. I could easily pick out veggies or the big cans of meat. But I could spot a tin of condensed milk from 10 yards away.

Raisin polished off the last of the leftovers and I started walking the long sand beach to see what might have floated in on the tide. Not much today. The ocean side was always better. I was always on the lookout for something useful even though my marauding of the boat left me in good shape.

"Maybe I'll find some shorts that blew off someone's boat, eh?" I look around and Raisin is pounding through the shallows. I think she's cornered a baby shark, judging by the dark, floppy fin just above the waves.

I start to sing like no one is listening. "Oh, what a beautiful morning …. Oh, what a beautiful day… I can't remember the damn words… everything's going my way." I may have hit the right notes. Or not.

I've spent many hours of many days trying to remember song lyrics, never my strong suit. I'll wander along the beach belting out "Sweet Caroline, good times never seemed so good…" one of my all time favorite. For other songs, if I can remember the tune, I make up the words as I go. The only ones I really remember are Christmas carols even though Jimmy Buffett is much more fitting for my surroundings.

I reach the end of the strand and turn back. It's not the day to plow through the shallows to the little pink island. It's interesting with a couple of long-abandoned houses and more open than "my" island, but I'm settled in.

I scan the tide. It's low so it could be a nice day to visit the reefs, I think. I quicken my pace to go pick up my snorkel and mask. The tide will be coming in so I won't need a safety line. I have a small anchor with a fender that I carry with me offshore so I have something to hang onto if I need it.

On rougher days I tie a 300-foot float line around my waist and fasten it to a mangrove.

Today I'm looking forward to a nice game with Mr. Turtle. And I need to check on the starfish, see how much progress she's making. The water is still warm from summer, but not for much longer. It truly is a beautiful day.

# MIKE

# CHAPTER 72

# October 15, afternoon

On his last night at Acklins, Mike moved the boat to the southern end ready to hang a U-turn and head for Samana. He hoped the wind would veer to make it a spinnaker run, but doubted he'd be that lucky.

In the meantime, he had lobsters in the freezer, fresh veggies in the fridge and a whole stalk of bananas ready to turn ripe. He didn't need fresh provisions for at least a couple of weeks.

He rose with the sun and motored around the tip of the island before activating the autopilot and raising the sails. Perfection. He steered the right course and adjusted the sails.

Wing on wing and sailing steady as a pool table. I'll be there in time for cocktails, he thought, eyeing the brand new rum bottle waiting in the corner of the cockpit.

Mike was making great time and turned on the autopilot so he could go forward with his binoculars to see if he could make out the low island. He could make out a smudge of trees on the horizon and his GPS told him he was about an hour away. That made for a perfect time to navigate into the anchorage with the high sun and flat water.

He stood for a while in the bow, relishing the wind in his hair and the prospect of exploring a real desert island. Samana was so far from anywhere else it only attracted the rare sport fisherman. No footprints but his own.

An hour later as he closed on the anchorage, he examined the small bay edged by a mangrove forest. He swept the shore with his binoculars and saw what looked like blankets in the trees near the edge of a white beach.

"Well, that's weird," he said it out loud. He decided to scout the island at a distance before pulling in. He sailed to within a quarter mile of the beach, binoculars trained on the mangroves. "Those sure look like blankets," he said. A hundred yards further on, he saw what looked like an Indian teepee a short distance from the mangroves.

"What the hell?" Out loud again. I better watch that, he said in his head, I sound nuts.

Druggies? Shit!

"That's the last thing I want in my little slice of paradise," he grumbled, "a bunch of drugged up pirates in the middle of the night… and it's too late to hole up anywhere else."

He scanned the long beach again and saw… a dog? A pretty big dog running in the water? And behind the dog, a person. A woman? Naked?

"Oh my god, this is surreal," out loud again. He couldn't help it.

He realized suddenly he was nearly on top of the reef, and could see dark patches way too close to the boat. He walked back to the cockpit, turned the boat into the wind and engaged the autopilot so he could drop the sails.

He winched the fluttering sails in, then went to the mast to release the halyard. He quickly bundled the sails and returned to the cockpit to turn back to the island.

He put the binoculars to his eyes again and now both the woman and the dog were running along the beach. She stopped once to face the boat and waved her arms over her head.

"My god, she's stark naked!" He couldn't believe his eyes, but she looked real all right. In pretty good shape, too. For a brief moment he felt like he'd never seen a naked woman before… he'd seen dozens, but they were usually in his bedroom. Or hotel room. And none of them looked like that! My god, she's like a mermaid with legs! She stopped again, this time gesturing him toward the mangrove end of the island.

He watched as she and the dog reached the teepee. She went inside and emerged wearing some sort of dress. A sarong. He couldn't tell what else. She had amazing hair. She looked like an Indian.

Maybe she's there for some ritual. But that teepee… it looks like it's covered with a sail.

The woman stood and waved again, then he heard a bad air horn. It sounded strangled. She pointed toward the mangroves, back the way he had come, toward the entrance to the anchorage he had passed by.

# ISLAND

# CHAPTER 73

# October 15, afternoon

The day passed like so many others.

If I weren't stranded, it would be perfection, I think.

As I walk along the edge of the water, I still look for perfect shells. Only the perfect ones now. I've picked up so many that I thought were perfect but found chips or oil spots … I finally made a little mountain with them. I still have way too many that stood the test, but I don't hear anybody telling me to stop.

Raisin's barks interrupt my thoughts. She must be tormenting that baby shark again, I think. She better hope his mom doesn't show up. She'll lose that nose for sure!  But her barks sound more urgent. I glance up and see a big catamaran, sails spread, practically on the beach!

"Raisin! Where the hell did that boat come from? Do they see us?!"

Holy shit, I stop cold and madly wave my arms. I can see a guy standing on the deck. He must see us! Christ! I'm naked! Well, at least I'm skinny now! Shit! He's got to stop! Does he have binoculars?

I start racing for the teepee, mostly out of modesty but partly because he's missed the anchorage and needs to turn around. I stop and wave again so he knows I'm serious. This time I'm waving him in. I'm doing my best Italian.

I reach the teepee and duck in to find a cover-up. I had salvaged clothes from 'Bama but none stay on. I had made a couple of sarongs from a cut-up sheet that I would wear for special occasions, like the nights I put a slash through the lines on the calendar tree, marking another week. Or the rare days I felt like I'd had enough sun.

"It's not pretty, but at least it covers most of me up, right, Raisin?" That tail is wagging faster than I thought possible. "We're gonna have a guest!"

I also grab the faulty air horn and hope for the best.

I race back outside. The guy has dropped the sails, thank god. He's going to stop. I wave again and point toward the anchorage. The air horn is balky but finally emits a hoarse screech like an angry camel.

He's in the cockpit now and is waving back at me and pointing to the anchorage. He looks pretty cute. Beard, hair, nice chest. He passes the 50-yard test.

"Hey Raisin, is our rescuer a hunky guy or not? Whaddaya think? Sign him up for tryouts?

"You dirty girl! You don't even know his name yet!" Raisin is sitting in the sand, blocking my way. Her yellow eyes tell me I'm acting nuts.

"It's ok, Raisin. We're going to meet a new friend. Friend? Right?"

I go back into the teepee for my reef shoes, then start on the well-trodden path toward 'Bama. With luck, his boat is shallow enough to anchor near the beach and I won't have to slog through the muck.

As I near the end of the sand beach I see the mast close on the shore, then reverse and stop. He's in. He must have a stern anchor out as well. I smile, glad I haven't forgotten the basics.

I stop walking. I'm nervous. Terrified, in fact. I haven't seen a human in… how many slashes now? Only three months? It feels like a lifetime! And this human will save my life! Unless he's some weirdo killer kidnapper. But I can't think about that.

I hope my sarong covers my naked ass and I walk to the edge of the sand where I can see the boat. Sweet, a big sailing catamaran, looks well kept. He's launching his dinghy. Shit, the guy's a Greek god. He's golden brown. All over? I wonder.

"Look at him, Raisin," I whisper. "If he rescues us, I can think of a lot of ways to say thank you. Shhh. Don't tell him that. He'll think I'm a slut.

"Does he have ice cream in that pretty boat? A freshwater shower? Oh my god, I'm already measuring for drapes. Mrs. Greek God is probably inside the cabin, curling her hair or plucking something. Doing her nails. Sluicing SPF 500 on herself because she's afraid of the sun."

Mr. Greek God starts the motor, then looks to see where I am. He grins and waves. Definitely cute. Nice smile. He slowly cruises over, standing so he can keep his eye on the depth, and noses the dinghy onto the sand.

I'm frozen in space and time. Raisin runs to him and gives him the new friend treatment of licks and wags. He bends to give her some rubs, then walks the 20 feet to me.

He stretches out his hand. "Hi, I'm Mike. Have you been here long?"

#

**Page 165**

The author is an intrepid sailor and traveler, a lifelong journalist and editor, a tilter at windmills and ruffler of feathers.

She divides her time between Vero Beach, Florida, for the ocean, and Phoenix, Arizona, for the mountains and desert.

She now travels with her aging dog and feral cat. She no longer answers Cruising World ads.

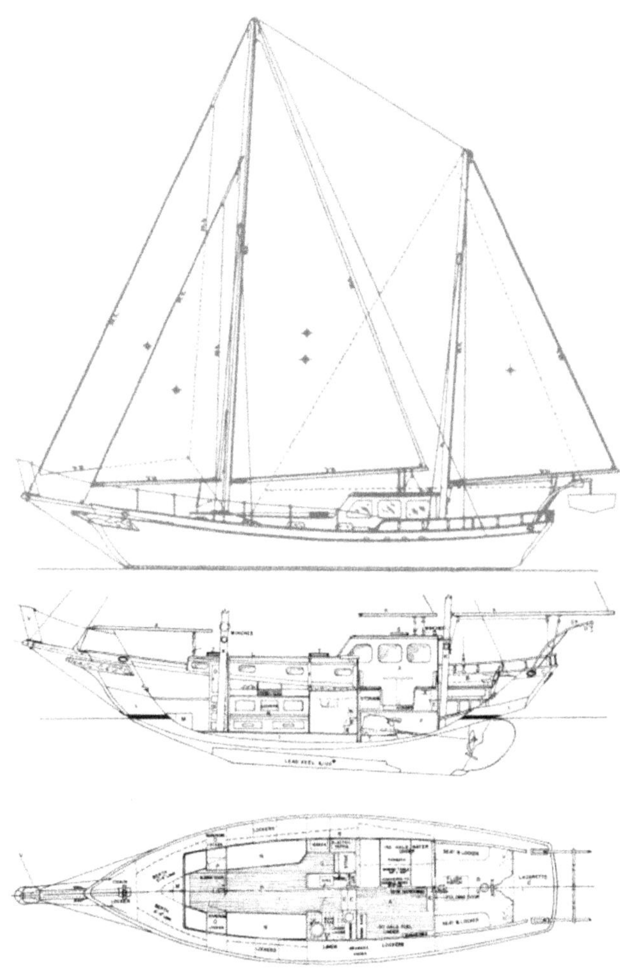